If We Must Die

....

....

....

....

....

...

Pat Carr

A Chaparral Book For Young Readers

IF WE MUST DIE

A novel of Tulsa's 1921
Greenwood riot

....

by Pat Carr

TCU Press
Fort Worth,

Copyright © 2002 Pat Carr

Library of Congress Cataloging-in-Publication Data

Carr, Pat M., 1932-
If we must die : a novel / by Pat Carr
p.cm. – (Chaparral books for young readers)
Summary: When seventeen-year-old, white Berneen O'Brien moves to
Tulsa and takes a job at a segregated elementary school,
she becomes increasingly involved in the lives of her black colleagues
and shares their experiences during the deadly race riot
that destroys Greenwood in 1921.
ISBN 0-87565-262-X paper
[1. Schools—Fiction. 2. African Americans—Fiction. 3. Tulsa (Okla.)—
Race relations—Fiction. 4. Riots—Fiction.] I. Title. II.
Chaparral book for young readers

PZ7.C22985 If 2002
[fic]—dc21   2001054837

cover illustration and design by
Barbara M. Whitehead

Printed in Canada

To the people of Greenwood,
who endured.

With many thanks

to Hannalore, who introduced me to the
International Women's Writing Guild
and the scores of friends I cherish,
to Stephanie and Cora, who tirelessly read
and re-read this manuscript,
to Angela, who bravely suggested I throw away
the initial version, and
to Duane Carr,
without whom I'd be lost.

If We Must Die

If we must die, let it not be like hogs
Hunted and penned in an inglorious spot,
While round us bark the mad and hungry dogs,
Making their mock at our accursed lot.
If we must die, O let us nobly die,
So that our precious blood may not be shed
In vain; then even the monsters we defy
Shall be constrained to honor us though dead!
O kinsmen we must meet the common foe!
Though far outnumbered let us show us brave,
And for their thousand blows deal one death blow!
What though before us lies the open grave?
Like men we'll face the murderous, cowardly pack,
Pressed to the wall, dying, but fighting back!

—Claude McKay (1919)

ONE

· · · · · · · · · ·

She crossed the railroad tracks and walked three blocks before she found it. A little whitewashed, two-story building with lots of hard-scrubbed windows and a wooden sign over the door with neatly painted block letters: LIBERTY ELEMENTARY SCHOOL.

She stopped and took a shaky breath.

Her first real job.

Children's shouts echoed from the fenced-in playground behind the schoolhouse, but no one was out front except a black gardener, kneeling, clipping the August grass.

He looked up and tugged his hat brim toward her. "'Morning, miss."

She hadn't seen many black people in her life—none, in fact, in Salt Creek, Wyoming. A well-dressed black woman, wearing a stylish hat and veil, had sat in the seat opposite when the train left Casper. As soon as they crossed into Oklahoma, the conductor came by and told the woman to move to the Jim Crow car.

Berneen hadn't wanted to stare, so she'd looked away while the woman adjusted her veil, gathered up her purse and *The New York Times,* and left.

Since she didn't want to gawk at the old gardener either, she merely nodded as she went up the steps and into the little schoolhouse.

The empty hallway smelled of wax, and she softened the tap of her high heels as much as she could until she saw PRINCIPAL on a brass oval beside a door.

She stopped and inhaled again while she knocked.

"Come in." It was a deep masculine voice.

She'd been expecting a woman.

The teachers in Salt Creek had been women, all but one instructor at her normal school had been women, all her classmates had been girls, and since the letter accepting her as the sixth-grade teacher had been signed "N.E. Flowers," she'd assumed the blossomy name belonged to a female.

She waited with her hand raised.

Then she reminded herself that it was, after all, 1920, and she'd arrived in a city of seventy-five thousand people.

Of course, some school officials might be men. Even an elementary school principal could be a man.

She pushed open the door.

The blinds were down, and a dimly visible man sat behind a desk.

Despite the dusk, however, she could tell he was tall and very dark. His shirt collar shimmered white, but his jacket, his tie, his face and hands glowed in shades of bittersweet chocolate, and his close-cropped hair had the firm matte finish of velvet.

He was black.

She was glad the shades were drawn since she knew her

face must be registering something—dismay, shock, something—even though she managed to keep her jaw from dropping in astonishment.

The man stood up, and through the gloom she could see a wide, deep scar under his right eye. "I'm Nelson Flowers. I assume you're Berneen O'Brien."

The question gave her a chance to nod, but she couldn't collect herself enough to say anything.

"You look somewhat like the snapshot you sent." He sat back down, and the swivel of his chair squeaked. His chocolate hand, with a palm that showed pale rose in the murky illumination, riffled some shadowy papers, and she recognized her application letter. "I was sorry to hear about your mother," he said. "I suppose it was unexpected."

She gaped at him, barely able to keep from blurting, "You're black!" But finally she faltered, "I guess blood poisoning is always unexpected."

"*Bien alors,*" he said. "Then we're lucky one of my teachers unexpectedly eloped with a jazz musician, aren't we?"

She'd had enough high school French to suspect he was making fun of her. But she stood there, too rattled to come up with a rejoinder.

How could someone black become a school principal in a place that sent black people to Jim Crow railway cars?

He was going on as if he hadn't expected an answer. "You're in Room 201. We assigned the older kids the second floor because we thought they'd be safer climbing the stairs. But we didn't realize how inventive they'd be about finding things to drop out the windows. So remember not to bring anything smaller than a chaise lounge to school with you."

Now she knew he was joking, but she couldn't think of anything clever—or even intelligible—to say.

"Why don't you go up and look at the room? I'm waiting for a call." He gestured through the twilight toward the licorice-colored pedestal and receiver on his desk as if he thought she might not recognize a telephone. "Stop by the office before you leave if you have any questions."

She could tell he'd already concluded she was a dunce.

But she nodded, backed out, pulled the door shut, and stumbled toward the stairs at the end of the hall. She clutched her purse with one hand, the banister with the other, and asked herself if the encounter in the shrouded office could have been a hoax.

Maybe a janitor had sat down at the desk pretending to be Principal N.E. Flowers. And maybe he'd been joshing her. About everything—including the job. His caustic use of French sounded like the whole thing might be a prank.

But he had been wearing a suit and tie.

And his sarcasm probably indicated some kind of authority.

She held the slick banister with a white-knuckled grip.

No, she decided as she climbed another dizzy step, it probably hadn't been a joke. But could the man in the office actually be the principal?

She reached the second floor.

Great blocks of sunlight spilled into the hall, and the door to Room 201 stood ajar at the top of the stairs. She could see the windows open to the sun and to child laughter from the yard.

Odors of linseed oil and bleach hung in the air.

A blackboard covered the wall behind the teacher's desk, a dozen small desks lined the center, and a child-sized table sat under the windows. Chalk and erasers hadn't been put out yet, books and crayons were still locked away in a closet somewhere, but everything else repeated exactly the school-room she'd pictured in her head.

She approached one of the windows and looked out at the playground.

A brass school bell dangled from a whitewashed pole in the center of the fenced yard, a whitewashed outhouse stood in the corner, and half a dozen little boys, of perhaps eight or nine, raced around the dirt lot.

One boy, his eyes covered by a red gingham kerchief, held out his arms while the others zigzagged close, then darted off in a careening game of blind-man's bluff. They ran barefooted, and as they ducked past the blindfolded boy, they kicked up a fringe of dust that grayed their feet and legs.

She stared down at them dodging and squealing below the window.

Their little feet and ankles might be gray, but their sweating arms and faces glistened like polished mahogany, and all of them wore their hair closely shorn like the man downstairs.

Of course the man she'd met was the principal.

She'd taken a job in a black school.

TWO

••••••••••

"Miss, can you join your uncle for dinner?"

The late afternoon sun glistened on the woman's gold-brown forehead and starched cotton apron.

Berneen could hear echoes of disdain from her uncle, whom she'd met the night before and who wasn't at all like her mother, and she toyed with refusing. Why should she try to be pleasant when he'd been so cold and distant? But she hadn't eaten a mouthful all day—and since the invitation included food—she told herself she might as well not be contrary about how, or why, she'd been invited to dinner.

So she produced a smile and a stiff, "Thank you."

She knew the woman, whose name was Ivory, served as cook and maid for her uncle and slept in a room beside the kitchen. Someone had sheared the lawn into a green rug, had cubed the hedges, and had shaped the trees beside the porch into silly topiary balls, so she guessed her uncle also hired a gardener. The burnished Ford touring car, parked in the garage under her loft room, might also indicate a chauffeur, but Ivory, with her black dress and white apron, was the only person Berneen had seen at the house besides her uncle.

Ivory stood at the threshold as if she expected something else, so Berneen murmured, "You can tell Uncle Quinn I'll be right down."

"Yes, miss." She pulled the door shut again, and her steps descended the outside stairs to the driveway.

Ever since Berneen had returned from the school, she'd sat on the white iron bed in the triangle-roofed room and tried to concentrate.

Liberty Elementary was a black school.

How could she teach there? In what she now knew was a segregated part of Tulsa?

How could she tell one black child from another?

What if everyone resented her because she was white?

She stared at the sloping white walls, at the fan-shaped window above the door, at the white enameled armoire and washstand beside the door, while the questions revolved in her skull like a squirrel in a cage.

Of course, she didn't have any answers.

But for the first time since she'd come, she did have a chance to eat. And she was starved. Images of bread and cheese and apples urged her off the bed while she decided that maybe she could think better after she ate.

And maybe, just maybe, she could find an opening to bring up her dilemma to her uncle.

She pressed the wrinkles from the white chenille bedspread and bent down to retrieve her new rhinestone-buckled shoes.

Her instep ached, but she told herself that if her mother

could contort her toes into the shape of a corncob, into the kind of footbinding disfigurement necessary to wear elegant quadruple-A alligator shoes, she could keep up some appearance of gentility while she stayed in the room over her uncle's garage.

So she wriggled her feet into the high heels and tottered over to the armoire where she'd hung her mother's fur coat when she'd arrived the night before.

She opened the mirrored door and held the fur sleeve to her cheek a second, the way she'd done sometimes even when her mother was alive. Then she smoothed the sleeve back in place, closed the armoire door, and glanced in the mirror at the dark waves of her hair before she went outside.

As she entered the back door and crossed the hall, she saw that the dining room table had been transformed with a snowy cloth and a centerpiece of red roses between two branched candlesticks. A dozen candles blazed and dripped wax over the silver candelabra even though bulbs in the electric chandelier glittered from the surfaces of the buffet and from her uncle's balding head.

His face at the head of the table radiated a summer sunburn as he removed his pince-nez—which left purple indentations beside his nose—and stared at her.

He made no pretense of rising. "I thought we should have dinner and get acquainted."

She didn't relish getting any better acquainted with him than she already was, but she didn't say that. She merely elevated her chin, sat down, and slipped the napkin from its silver ring just as Ivory came in with two plates of soup.

Three discs of carrot, one bright green pea, and a twig of parsley floated in the transparent broth.

She noticed her uncle's eyes—dark brown, but not as dark as her own—still staring as she lifted her spoon. He picked up his own spoon, and she realized he must have wanted to see if she resembled her late mother rather than if she knew the polite way to eat soup. Since he himself didn't seem to know he was supposed to drag the soupspoon backward through the broth, she relaxed and said, "This has a nice flavor."

"Ivory's a good cook. She's been with me since I got mustered out," her uncle said. "She's from Langston." He returned the pince-nez to his nose, and the lenses immediately became little mirrors reflecting the candlelight. "At first she served the kind of food darkies eat, but I managed to break her of that habit."

Berneen swallowed the spoonful of soup.

So much for her dilemma.

But since the meal might be her last for some time—and it had been offered free—she grasped the soupspoon and told herself sternly to stay put. She nonetheless cut off any further discussion of "darkies" by saying calmly, "Mama said you went overseas during the war."

"I survived the Great War in France for a year, four months, and nineteen days."

She might have quipped, "But who's counting?" if she'd been sitting at the table with anyone except this stranger who was her uncle, but as it was, she threw him another safe comment. "I thought lawyers in the oil business could stay out of the army."

"I volunteered. It had to do with 'patriotism.' Which is a concept no one understands any longer. Just as no one understands what war is like."

His sour-cherry complexion deepened to maroon.

"My wife didn't stay around to try to understand. While I lay in the hospital with a wounded leg, she bobbed her hair, learned to fox-trot, and ran off with some slacker of a gigolo."

Berneen resisted the impulse to touch her own bobbed hair.

"Divorce should have been outlawed when they outlawed liquor," he said.

She decided he'd resolved to needle her about her mother since he had to know she'd been divorced twice, and she debated whether to defend her mother or to let it go.

Before she'd decided, Ivory carried in plates of pink beef and potatoes smothered in cream gravy.

Her uncle took up his heavy sterling knife and fork.

Free food was one thing, but Berneen told herself she could do without it if she had to swallow too much humble pie with the mashed potatoes. So she said, "I've always thought if people weren't happy together, they should go find someone they could be happy with."

"Happiness is an illusion." He began to chop his entire serving of beef into bite-sized chunks as if he intended to stuff it down a toddler. "My ex-wife expected someone else to make her happy, but she's miserable."

"And you'd rather she'd stayed to be miserable with you?"

He did a persimmon thing with his mouth and retreated into a lawyer's trick. "Was your mother happier after she divorced that first one, that Albert Swinny?"

"Alfred."

Alfred Swinny had fathered her, but since her mother had left him before her birth and had inked her own maiden name on the birth certificate, Berneen had never seen him.

"Of course she was happier," she said stoutly. "He was a drunk and a wife-beater. Why should a woman stay in that situation if she could escape?"

"She made a contract."

She'd devoured the soup, had sampled the potatoes, and she could forego the rare beef if she had to.

So she said, "Bosh."

She'd have stared down his eyes if they hadn't been hidden behind those mirror glasses. "You sound like a character out of *Jane Eyre*." It was the tone her mother always called mouthy. "It's lame nowadays to insist someone stay married simply because they bought the license. If no one warned you the person you married would become insane and violent or drunk and violent, I think there's a whale of a loophole in the contract."

He forked up a mince of beef. "Eileen should have known not to marry a black Irishman who drank. Our father should have taught her that."

Berneen had never seen her black-haired, swarthy grandfather either, so she shrugged. "Mama had a profession. She had the means to get out of a bad situation, so I, for one, don't see why she should have stayed."

"Eileen was a nurse. She didn't have a profession; she had a trade. But at least she encouraged you to get enough education to teach." He chewed and swallowed another cube of beef. "Even if you do seem too young to have a teacher's certificate."

She raised her chin. "I'm seventeen."

"Oh." He opened his mouth about to add something else, but just then a jet-black cat jumped onto his lap.

Her Uncle Quinn didn't seem like someone who would own a pet or would countenance having one at the table, but he stroked the cat and held out the final bite of meat to it as he looked back at Berneen. "I hope, however, you realize how fortunate you are to have found a job. We came back after the 1918 armistice expecting boom times, but instead we hit a bust."

The rock that was balanced near the top of her stomach dropped.

She held the oversized dinner fork, kept the hand in her lap from twitching, and tried for an expression to indicate that she knew all about the post-war recession.

"There was no work for veterans who risked their lives in the war, let alone for women who shouldn't be in the workplace, taking jobs from men."

She sat facing him and the ebony cat, but she didn't focus on them.

She'd taken a job that should have gone to a man.

A black man.

THREE

· · · · · · · · · · · ·

She hunched against the curve and spokes of the white iron bed and stared at the walls.

She had nowhere else to go. She had to stay for the time being with this uncle who was her only living relative.

"You could have checked with me, Mac, before you wrote to Uncle Quinn," she'd said when Mac had knocked on the door, sheepish, holding out her uncle's letter.

"The company's going to reassign this shack now that Eileen's not working for the camp hospital. You've finished two years of college, and there's nothing for you here. The least I could do for Eileen was to find you some place to go."

It had been no secret that her mother wanted to marry him, and *that* would have been the least he could do. But since her mother was dead and Mac had stood there with her uncle's offer of a room and she had to leave Salt Creek anyway, she said she'd go to Tulsa and find a job.

She had found a job.

And after scouring want ads in the *Tulsa World* all week-end, she knew she could either show up at Liberty Elementary on Monday or she could tell her uncle what had happened and beg him to let her hole up over his garage for the next six months while she looked for other employment.

It wasn't a choice.

So Monday morning, she walked numbly downtown to catch the trolley.

She stood beside the yellow-brick Drexel Building at the trolley stop and read a banner strung across Main Street. "Welcome to the Magic City." It had sagged on its lanyards.

As she glanced away from it, she saw a water fountain jutting from the building wall. The drinking fountain was actually just a sink and a spigot turning green at the joints, but someone had attached a sign, "White Only," to the bricks above the faucet.

Had she waited at the same spot on Friday?

If she had, she certainly hadn't noticed the cardboard warning. But now the black letters seared themselves into her brain, and she stared at them while a hollow in her rib cage expanded to constrict her lungs.

By the time the trolley pulled up she felt woozy from lack of air.

She handed the driver her nickel, crowded into the aisle with other sweating people, and while the tram swayed along, she tried to think.

She hadn't fused two thoughts, however, before the driver announced, "Greenwood coming up," and she elbowed her way to the door and climbed down to the sidewalk.

A black woman, carrying a maid's uniform over one arm, exited from the back door at the same time, and when the trolley clattered off again, it dawned on Berneen that passengers in the front were white and those jammed into the last row were black.

She hadn't noticed that on Friday either.

She let the woman cross the railroad track and gain the next block while she slowed her pace to prepare herself.

But it was no use. She didn't know what to prepare herself for.

Abruptly, she arrived at the little schoolhouse again.

A middle-aged black woman was herding children with ironed clothes and neatly tied shoes through the fence gate to the play yard, and Berneen was relieved that they seemed too anxious about their own first day to notice her arrival.

She went up the steps behind a gray-haired man—also too preoccupied with straightening the celluloid collar around his mahogany neck to glance at her as she eased inside—and she made it to Room 201 without meeting anyone.

The room sat sunny, spotless—and vacant—just as it had been before.

The one bit of busywork she'd planned all the way from Casper had been to write her name on the board and introduce herself to the class, but now she couldn't see any chalk.

She pulled out the desk drawers, one after the other, and felt inside every drawer. They were completely empty.

She shut them again and flattened her twitching fingers against the polished desktop. Waves of despair eddied around her.

"Isn't it beastly hot today?" A tall, coffee-colored girl with broad shoulders materialized in the doorway.

She sopped a handkerchief over pencil-arched eyebrows and the bridge of a prominent, hooked nose while she said,

"You're from Wyoming, aren't you?" She loomed on the threshold, dazzling in a white dress, silver squash-blossom necklace, hoop earrings, silver bracelets circling both arms, and a ring on every finger. "Lord love a duck, but you're a little bit of a thing."

Although the girl topped Berneen by no more than an inch, she filled the doorway with her black hair swept into a Gibson Girl pouf and her shirtwaist that reached from her chin to the laces of her old-fashioned oxfords.

The second Berneen saw the long skirt, buttoned-at-the-wrist sleeves, and sensible shoes, she knew that she herself was dressed all wrong.

"No one had a clue Rima would run off with that saxophonist from Memphis. Would you believe she knew him only a week? My daddy'd kill me if I did something like that. But isn't it too romantic? How did Mr. Flowers find you at the last minute? Can you imagine a herd of sixth-grade urchins loose in here without a teacher?"

If she'd expected a reply, Berneen might have confessed that she'd seen the ad almost accidentally and that she didn't know much about sixth-graders since she'd skipped that grade when she'd been in school.

But the girl in the doorway didn't expect a reply, and she rapid-fired more information, embedded like raisins in her questions, as she strode in and extended a sturdy hand. "Have you found a place to stay yet? My daddy's got the real estate office on Archer Avenue, and he'll know some rooms for rent. I bet your hometown wasn't this hot, was it? I'm Caroline Mankiller. I'm next door with the fourth and fifth graders."

Berneen blinked against the girl's sparkling eagerness and tried to keep her own voice from wavering as she stepped from behind the desk and took the hand held out to her. "I'm Berneen O'Brien."

Caroline Mankiller may not have heard her name as she gasped at Berneen's knee-length skirt, stockings, and rhinestone-buckled shoes. "Lord love a duck, don't you look swell! Why didn't I get the figure to wear something smart like that?"

Berneen's cheeks grew warm. "I guess I didn't pack anything but short skirts."

"Oh, don't worry, the fuddy-duddies around here could stand to see some style! I'd wear a sexy flapper outfit, too, if I hadn't inherited my great-granddaddy's running legs as well as his beak." She grimaced and tapped her nose. "And his ridiculous name. I just wish Great-granddaddy had been a sensible southern planter with a sensible name like Taylor or Jackson instead of Mankiller."

Berneen could tell from the prideful way she said the name and from the Indian jewelry encasing her like chain mail that she didn't wish anything of the kind.

"Or if my name had to be Mankiller, why couldn't it be indicative of my love life?" She released Berneen's hand and added, "But wouldn't you know? I'm so far from slaying men with my beauty or intelligence that I'm nineteen and still an old maid." Her eyes crinkled beneath the drawn-on eyebrows, and a grin flashed beneath the out-of-place nose. "I tell myself it doesn't help that I'm the youngest of seven. Are you married?"

Berneen shook her head.

"Well then, we've got to stick together until we find Mr. Tall-Dark-and-Handsome. This is my second year here, and I know what makes the wheels go around, so if you need anything—"

She didn't exactly pause, but she inhaled, and Berneen threw in quickly, "The janitor didn't leave me any chalk. Do you think I have time to go to the office and get some before class?"

Caroline Mankiller readjusted the necklace that could have served as a breastplate. "Girl, the office doesn't have chalk. Would you believe they pay us the princely sum of eight hundred dollars a year and expect us to buy our own chalk?" She gave her skirt a kick as she turned to leave. "I've got a brand-new stick. I'll lend you half."

Berneen's throat tightened with gratitude.

With staccato cheerfulness, Caroline Mankiller had dropped confidences most people kept from strangers, and now she offered to share her chalk. She evidently didn't mind that Berneen was white.

Berneen took a breath and followed her.

"I love greenery. Don't you?" Caroline had already started talking. "I'll get you some cuttings. My Aunt Belle has the greenest thumb in Adair County." She waved her rings at ivy sprouting from Mason jars along the windowsill, then swung a silver-bedecked hand toward a calendar advertising Jackson's Undertaking Company. "I'll get you one of those, too. The picture could be cheerier, couldn't it? Who needs to be reminded a funeral is waiting down the street?"

Under the grainy photograph of a top-hatted, dark-faced man beside a black hearse, that day's date, September 3, 1920, had been circled in red.

"But the calendar's free, so I suppose we can't complain, can we?" She swooped a length of chalk off the desk, broke it, and held out a half.

Berneen didn't know how to thank her—for the chalk or

for her acceptance—and she said lamely, "I've never taught before."

"Oh, I knew that. But don't worry, the little pests will adore you. You won't have any trouble."

Berneen couldn't ask if she had any trouble telling the little pests apart.

Nor could she ask anything else as the clang of an alarm suddenly filled the room.

Someone urgently banged a tin spoon against an iron pan.

Berneen looked at Caroline Mankiller startled.

"That's the school bell," Caroline yelled over the sound. "One of the urchins gets to pull the rope every morning and afternoon. You'll get used to it." She straightened two silver blossoms in her necklace and shooed with a big hand while she shouted, "Now go write your name on the board."

Berneen got to the room and began chalking her name as children pushed through the door, keeping their eyes downcast as they stood lumped shyly together.

Then, with thunderclap abruptness, the bell stopped.

In the deafening silence, Berneen had to do something, and she said, in a tone she hoped sounded adult, "Please find a seat."

She lifted her chin, leveled her eyes toward the children as if she saw them, and told them her name. Then she added, "I'm going to assign desks in alphabetical order. When I pass around paper and pencil, I want you to write your names clearly."

Only then did she realize the single piece of paper in the room was her letter of acceptance from Principal Nelson Flowers, and the single stub of a pencil was the one she'd carried in her purse from Salt Creek.

She got them from the little silk bag, pretending she'd brought them especially for the children, and smoothed the letter facedown on a desk.

She held out the pencil nubbin to a little girl, who bent at once to print, "Vivian Green."

Berneen composed herself enough to focus.

Vivian Green, slumping in an awkward satin dress cut down from a woman's slip, had a Hershey bar complexion and a multitude of black-yarn plaits. The next girl, with the glow of fresh nutmeg, sat up straight in a puff-sleeved, yellow gingham. The boy behind her had arrived in a miniature suit complete with tie and vest, while the round, ginger-colored boy beside him strained the seams of his overalls like an overstuffed sofa bolster. The tallest boy, Sam Rollins, who sat gazing out the window, could have been cast from bronze. He was all elbows and knees and too angular to be wedged into a stunted desk.

They came in shades of walnut, hickory, and copper. Their eyes swerved timidly around the room in medicine-bottle brown, obsidian, and amber. Most had black hair, but one girl, as plump as the gingerbread boy, had carroty locks tumbling about her ears in corkscrew curls.

Berneen took a deep breath and watched them write their names on the back of her letter.

Of course she could tell them apart.

FOUR

When she left school that afternoon, she stopped at The Novelty Shop on Archer to buy a nickel's worth of chalk.

The woman behind the counter exclaimed, "What elegant shoes!" And as she took Berneen's nickel, she added with a friendly tilt of her head, "Nobody but a teacher or a seamstress be needing chalk."

"I'm a teacher—at Liberty Elementary."

The woman beamed. "Now, ain't that fine."

The sun glinted from a bone-clear sky, and Berneen wiped a palm across her sweating forehead while she stepped around the coal slag between the railroad ties and crossed to First Street. It was hot, but she happily dangled her purse by its chain and savored the fact that she'd made it through the day by having the children alphabetize, do sums on the board, and share what they liked best in the world to eat.

That evening, her uncle surprised her by renewing his

dinner invitation, and as she joined him at the table, he asked perfunctorily, "How was your day?"

"I have eleven well-behaved little kids, so eager to learn that—"

"I don't see that discussing how one civilizes small children makes particularly entertaining dinner conversation," he interrupted, showing with his curt dismissal that he had no desire to hear about what she was doing.

On her walk home, she'd wondered how to tell him she was teaching in a black neighborhood, but now she saw she needn't say a word about her job or the school if she didn't want to.

And she certainly didn't want to.

When her uncle gave the last chunk of his veal cutlet to the cat, which he called Black Jack Pershing after a general in the war, he said importantly, "I have a meeting this evening."

She waited until he went out the front door with his slight limp before she hurried to the kitchen.

Ivory glanced up from her dishpan. "Yes, miss?"

"Might something be left from dinner that—" She stopped and began again. "Is there possibly something I could take to school for lunch?"

Ivory seemed to study her with a dubious expression, and she wondered if her uncle had warned his cook that his niece might come around cadging food.

But then Ivory shook water off her hands and opened the pie safe. "I fix pone for myself." She lifted a tea towel from a pan of cornbread. "I don't suppose you'd be wanting that."

Berneen overrode her uncle's contempt for "darkie" food with an enthusiastic, "That would be great."

Ivory slid the pan onto the shelf again and returned to her dishes. "I can bundle some up for you tomorrow then."

Berneen returned to the loft room, turned on the overhead light, and tried to re-read a few pages from *Pride and Prejudice,* the one book she'd brought from Salt Creek.

But when she blinked and re-opened her eyes, sunlight streamed through the semi-circle of glass over the door.

"Where am I?" she said aloud. "What happened?"

She sat up bewildered under the slanting walls.

It was morning.

She whispered, "Oh, yes, Mama died. I'm at Uncle Quinn's."

Her lips quivered, but she got up, poured water from the washstand pitcher into the bowl, and splashed her face.

As soon as she got dressed, she snuggled her cheek against the fur coat a moment before she closed the armoire door, went out, and crossed the driveway to the kitchen.

A wrapped square of cornbread sat on the counter. She stuffed it into her purse and left without seeing anyone.

The morning had dawned almost cool, and she felt better as she walked through the residential area under the trees. Her mother had always nagged her to wear a hat or gloves in the sun—"You're getting so dark people will start to take you for a Gypsy"—but with all the shade trees in Tulsa, her mother wouldn't have worried about her getting any tanner.

She crossed into the business section with its yellow brick and sheltering glass marquees, and she'd nearly passed the *Tulsa World* building when she noticed a roll of blank newsprint in the trash bin.

One of her childhood diversions back in Salt Creek had been to hike to the town dump and search through discarded pillows, rusted cans, and half-emptied bottles for treasures. Once she'd found an entire, sealed box of candy, and while she and her mother ate the chocolates, her mother made up a story about a roustabout rejected by a beauty who threw out his gift unopened. Her mother's stories generally ended tragically, and, in that one, the broken-hearted suitor hanged himself from a rig in sight of the girl's house.

Berneen caught a glimpse of the trolley coming.

Just like that box of unspoiled candy, some printer had discarded that perfectly good roll of paper with the sweepings.

She stood looking at it.

A garbage bin probably qualified as a sort of minidump, but this was a city street rather than a hollow beside a sump hole, and she knew that respectable Tulsans wouldn't pluck items from trash cans.

But she wasn't a respectable Tulsan. And she could use that paper.

The trolley pulled up to the stop.

She flicked the roll off the pile, tucked it under her arm, and climbed the trolley steps.

Half a block from the school, she saw Caroline Mankiller waiting on the school porch

"I was afraid you were going to be late." Caroline ushered her to a first-floor room where a matronly woman—the woman Berneen had seen the day before—sat at a desk.

"This is Berneen O'Brien," Caroline said as they went in. "Doesn't she look adorable in those stockings and highheels? She's from Wyoming, and she's single. This is Persephone Ellsworth. She teaches the second grade. Persephone's husband, Zacharia, is the head butcher at York's Meat Market. Did Mr. Flowers mention that he's the first-grade teacher as well as the principal? He came to the school last year when I started, and he's not married, but then, I guess it'd be hard for him to find someone who could overlook that awful scar."

"Caroline!" Persephone Ellsworth chided. She had a full mouth of gold teeth except for the first molar, which retained its original white enamel. "You needn't be telling everybody's business just because you can't keep quiet about your own."

Caroline merely tossed her head and barreled on. "The only one you haven't met, Berneen, is Hanford Yarborough, with the third grade. He's my daddy's age, and he's a church deacon. His wife's bedridden, so he always looks sad and austere, and he's always spreading oil on troubled waters—whether they're troubled or not. But he's really a marsh-mallow inside, so try not to let his pessimism and his ill-omened advice get to you."

Then she caught sight of the blank newsprint. "Oh, you brought paper!"

"I rescued it from the trash—for the children to draw on," Berneen said at once. If there was anything she didn't want, it was for Caroline and Persephone Ellsworth to see her as a dilettante able to afford a roll of paper.

"Aren't you clever!" Caroline cried as the bell began its window-shaking din. "Why can't I think of things like that?"

"It's probably because you never stop talking long enough to think." Persephone Ellsworth raised her voice while she gave Berneen a conspirator's wink.

As she and Caroline climbed the stairs together under the clamor of the bell, Berneen was flooded with a sense of warmth and companionship.

Persephone Ellsworth had also accepted her.

After school that day, on the way to her uncle's, Berneen stopped at the same five-and-ten-cents store for two boxes of Crayolas, and the woman behind the counter beamed the same friendly smile as she dropped the boxes in a bag.

The next morning, the children gazed with reverence at the crayons while Berneen said in the adult voice she'd been practicing, "Work hard on your arithmetic and spelling reviews, and Friday we'll have creative time."

After a moment of silence, little Vivian Green asked softly, "What's 'creative time,' Miss O'Brien?"

"You'll have free time to draw pictures."

They stared solemnly another few seconds before Vivian Green asked, "We can draw whatever we want?"

"Whatever you want."

When Friday came, they waited patiently for her to pass out the Crayolas and then bent earnestly over their squares of paper, which she'd cut from the roll with scissors borrowed from her uncle's desk. And as the dismissal bell hammered through the school, she felt very grown up and accomplished.

No one could have done a better job with a first week of school.

She tripped happily downstairs to the office, where the window blinds had been raised. Nelson Flowers stood in a halo of sun, contemplating the street.

She hesitated at the door.

He continued to look out the window, but when he said, "Yes?" she knew he knew she stood there.

"I was wondering—" she began.

Something about Nelson Flowers discomfited her. Maybe it was his height, which had to be over six feet, or his age, which had to be twice hers, or perhaps merely his sarcasm. She fumbled into silence.

"Well?" He turned toward her.

He had eyes the perfect shape and size of peach pits with silvery corneas and black pupils indistinguishable from the surrounding near-black irises. They might have been fashioned of onyx and sterling to decorate an Egyptian tomb. As she registered their intensity, she also became acutely aware of the wound in his cheekbone, gouged as long and deep as a thumb. It was as if a space had been hollowed for a third eye.

"You undoubtedly came in for something," he prompted sarcastically.

She gaped at the scar tissue in the pocket of the wound that had healed pink and crisp. Then she swallowed and said in a rush, "I'm running out of reviews. I was wondering when we get this year's textbooks."

"Well, now, that's something we all wonder about, Miss O'Brien. The 'Wobblies' want to pass out free schoolbooks, but the state argues *fortement* that students worth educating can buy their own books."

She considered asking what "Wobblies" were, but he went on before she could. "The uptown schools purchase new textbooks every September. But our students must collect pennies from Mount Zion Baptist Church."

"To buy books?" She knew she sounded like a simpleton.

"*Certainement,* to buy books," he said with heavy sarcasm. "We never know when the collection plates will yield enough for an entire class, but I assume, Miss O'Brien, that you possess a modicum of information the average sixth-grader doesn't have. So why don't you just teach the children everything you know."

FIVE

·······

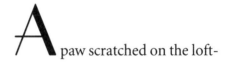A paw scratched on the loft-
room door.

Berneen opened the door to Black Jack Pershing, who
sauntered in and made a fluid leap onto the chenille spread.
He considered a moment, then curled into a puddle of fur
on the pillow.

"Did Uncle Quinn send you up to tell me dinner was
ready?"

She kicked off the buckled shoes, slipped out of the chiffon dress, and hung it beside her mother's fur. She tugged
the navy cotton off its hanger.

With her first paycheck, she'd start saving for an apartment, but she'd also have enough money to go into a store
and try on a ready-made dress—something she'd done only
once before in her life.

"The least I can do is buy you a traveling outfit," Mac
had said the morning she left Casper. "I couldn't get back

from the oil field in time for Eileen's funeral, but at least I can get you a dress to wear on the train."

Her mother had always created clothes from patterns she carried around in her head, and the short-skirted navy blue shift had been made from the bolt her mother took in trade for midwifing the Swenson's third baby. The style had come straight from an illustration in *Cosmopolitan,* and Berneen knew it was sophisticated.

But she also knew she could use a store-bought dress when she got to Tulsa, so she didn't balk at Mac's buying one for her. She merely stood at the counter and said, "Oh, look, Mac," while she pointed out a purse and shoes that went with the dress.

When he'd paid for the dress, the high heels, purse, and a waist-long strand of faux pearls—which the salesgirl insisted set off her olive skin—he drove her to the station, bought a train ticket with another sheaf of ten-dollar bills, and carried her mother's fur coat and her suitcase—which contained everything Berneen now owned—down the platform.

And right then, for the first time since she'd left Salt Creek, she experienced a great hole in her chest. She'd probably never see Mac again, and he was the last of her mother's men, the last of her mother. But she knew she would have acted like a baby if she'd tried to hug him or even give him a peck on the cheek. That's another thing she'd learned—that if you touched someone, the fragile net somewhere inside that held back the sobs would snap, and you'd end up bawling like a little kid.

So she'd been careful not to graze his hand as she took the ticket and the suitcase, hitched the coat over her shoulder, and climbed the metal steps to the vestibule between cars.

"Let me hear from you sometime," he said.

Fortunately the train had jerked to a start right away, and she could call, "Bye, Mac. Thanks," as if she were going on vacation and might even be coming back.

Now, in the loft room, she pulled the blue dress over her head.

Of course, she wouldn't be going back to Wyoming.

The cat watched her with serious, chartreuse eyes as she went out and left the door open for him.

During the week, at six every evening, she'd crossed the brick driveway, gone through the back hall, and wandered into the dining room, where the table was laid with two settings and where her uncle sat waiting.

Dinner conversation turned out to be much the same every evening. Her uncle would make pronouncements about the collapse of American values. "Too many people have already forgotten why America fought the war." Or complain about President Woodrow Wilson. And then with the soup course, he'd launch into a battlefield story. "No one could raise his head above the trench or he'd get it blown off."

She calculated that sooner or later he'd want to talk about something other than his experience in France, but since he supplied free meals while he talked, she told herself it was all right if he wanted to bring up the war every night. She could offer an occasional "M-m-m-m," sit quietly, and eat.

"I remember the dawn we went over the top as though it were yesterday," he began.

He told stories the way her mother always had—with the same pauses and identical hand movements.

"An officer tapped us on the back, and we climbed the

ladders. Then we ran through the fog and powder fumes to openings in the barbed wire. We ran until the fog lifted and the Huns sighted us in their machine guns. That's when men started dropping in the mud. A soldier with a great hole in his chest collapsed beside me, but I didn't stop."

Berneen watched him hack pork from his chop bone.

She'd listened to her mother's hospital stories about bodies mangled by gears or crushed in falls from catwalks, and once she'd even helped in the emergency room after a rig collapse. So she ate calmly through her uncle's battle-front details.

"We heard the bullets whining past. Over us, around us, whizzing, cracking against the wire, cutting into the dirt at our feet. There was nothing we could do but run." He stared over the centerpiece roses into the past. "No one under-stands the horror. No one knows what war does to a man."

Black Jack Pershing sprang into his lap.

"I was motivated by patriotism, but I lost opportunities for advancement. And when you come from the kind of background I had—" He broke off before he revealed some-thing personal.

Berneen knew all about him from her mother, but since he obviously didn't realize that, she maintained a protective silence while he fed Black Jack Pershing the last scrap of pork chop. Ivory came through the swinging door with dessert dishes of red Jell-O.

When her uncle didn't look up, Berneen guessed he'd finished reminiscing—and griping—for the evening, and she cleared her throat across the sputter of candle wax. "What are Wobblies?"

He scowled and knuckled the cat's silky head. "Where did you hear about Wobblies?"

Berneen knew he wouldn't want her to say that the black principal of her black school had mentioned them, so she kept quiet, and after a moment he said, "Wobblies are a festering swarm of anarchists. They want to undo everything we fought for in the war."

"I thought they wanted to give free textbooks to school children."

"That's what I mean." He frowned up from the cat. "Any child who should attend school can buy his own textbooks. Children too poor to afford books won't benefit from education. It's ridiculous to try to teach them."

"Mama told me you were dirt poor when you were kids."

"That was different. Being poor wasn't the same when we were children. We worked hard, gave an honest day's labor for an honest dollar, and those of us who wanted to learn found the money to buy books. Today the poor whine and call for strikes and wait for handouts."

His face reddened, and she could see she'd touched a nerve.

"We shouldn't send poor children to school or fill their heads with information that is useless to them. We need to educate children capable of learning." He gestured imperiously toward the bowl of roses. "American Beauties like those can bloom in full splendor only by sacrificing the less significant buds around them."

"In case you hadn't heard," Berneen said dryly, "the scent's been bred out of American Beauty roses, too."

Her uncle ignored that and pushed back his chair.

"The Wobblies want to drag the children of worthless

scum and minorities into our schools. They're even demanding equality for the coloreds."

Fortunately, he dropped the cat to the carpet just then, and Berneen could escape to the room above the garage.

The moon threw a pencil of silver light onto the slanted wall. It reminded her of Nelson Flowers' eyes.

Nelson Flowers towered straighter, a head taller—and, even with that scar, obviously more physically fit—than her stoop-shouldered uncle. But Nelson Flowers expected her to educate the sixth graders of Liberty Elementary whether or not she ever got a textbook.

She wished she could spin tales the way her mother—or her uncle—did, but since she wasn't a storyteller, she was going to need some of that "useless" information her uncle railed against.

She was going to need books.

Books from her uncle's library.

She watched the moonlight another minute, slipped off the high heels, and slid on the pair of carpet slippers she'd also rescued from the Salt Creek dump. They were nearly her size, and the only thing wrong with them was an unraveling embroidered rose on the toe of the left shoe.

The moon shone brighter than the streetlight in the alley, and she padded easily down the stairs, across the bricks, and into the back hall.

As far as she could tell, her uncle never used anything in the three-story house except the library, the dining room, and a room on the second floor that was his bedroom. She'd never seen him in the parlor, where the sofas overflowed with lace antimacassars and yellow satin pillows that matched the drapes, and where all the lampshades dripped bead fringe. She suspected his ex-wife had decorated it, and she wondered why her uncle didn't just throw everything out and start over.

She went past the parlor to the library.

The library was the snuggest room she'd ever been in, and she wished her mother could have seen it.

It contained floor-to-ceiling barrister bookcases, a huge oak desk, a burgundy leather sofa, and—in the middle of the wall over the desk—a stained-glass window with a red glass hand dead center.

The story of that scarlet hand, the Red Hand of Ulster, had been one of her mother's all-time favorites, and she'd heard countless times about the two Celtic earls racing their skiffs across the Irish Channel to win Ireland by being the first to touch land. When Ulster—whom her mother claimed as an ancestor—saw his boat falling behind, he grabbed his sword, cut off his own hand, and threw it onto the beach.

The second she'd seen the stained glass window, she knew her uncle needed those phony ancestors as much as her mother had. She knew he was as defensive as her mother about being poverty-stricken shanty Irish.

She sighed again.

Then she turned on the overhead light and went to the bookshelves.

Her uncle owned scores of leather-bound tomes on law, politics, philosophy, history, and eugenics. He had sets of encyclopedias, a row of *The Book of Knowledge,* and on a bottom shelf, dozens of novels, most of them by either Charles Dickens or Anthony Trollope.

She knelt down and took out *Great Expectations.*

Her uncle probably wouldn't miss it.

Then—after another scan of the shelves—she got out Volume I of Forsythe's *History of America.*

She could read the children a chapter a day from each book. After she gleaned biology and mathematics from the encyclopedias and *The Book of Knowledge,* she, with the help of Mr. Dickens and Mr. Forsythe, would replace a sixth-grade textbook.

She cradled the borrowed volumes with satisfaction while she diminished the gaps left by their absence, closed the shelf doors, and turned off the light.

Moonlight shone through the red glass hand to drop a blood-colored stain on the carpet. The muscles down her spine quivered just as they always had when her mother described the thud of that bloody, severed hand striking the Irish shore.

She backed into the hallway, onto the hardwood floor that felt icy through the soles of the slippers, and shuddered.

SIX
········

When she'd decided to give the children creative time, she told herself she wouldn't comment on their pictures no matter what they drew.

But the following Friday as she gave Beata Jackson—of the orangey corkscrew curls—a square of blank newsprint and a purple Crayola, she caught a glimpse of Vivian Green drawing Sam Rollins with a blue crayon.

It took all her control to hold her tongue.

But she clenched her jaw and moved down the row to look at the lopsided purple dog Beata had begun to render from faulty memory.

After the afternoon bell clanged, however, she stopped Vivian at the door. "What did you do with your picture of Sam, Vivian?"

Vivian started. "Sam don't mind, Miss O'Brien. In fact, he don't even see me looking at him. But I know staring ain't good, and I won't draw nobody if you don't want me to."

"I wasn't calling you down for staring." She sounded like her mother. "I just wanted to see your sketch."

Vivian gazed up a moment from eye sockets as dark as plums. Then she crept to her desk, lifted the lid, and carefully took out a newsprint scroll.

She shyly unrolled it.

The blue portrait of Sam was even better than Berneen had thought.

He sat languid and motionless, the way he usually lolled through the school day, and there was no mistaking his features or his dreamy expression. But under the stillness, Vivian had conveyed a sense that he sat coiled, ready to erupt. She'd omitted the too-small desk and depicted him lounging on what could have been a rock, a ledge, or a throne.

"How did you learn to do this?"

Vivian shrugged.

"Did anyone teach you to draw?"

She shrugged again.

"May I show this to Mr. Flowers?"

The little girl stared at the floor.

"I'd really like him to see it."

Finally, Vivian's scrawny shoulders raised and lowered, and she whispered, "I guess so."

She started for the door and murmured, "You keep that picture of Sam if you want, Miss O'Brien."

Berneen resisted the impulse to look at Vivian's other sketches as she closed the windows.

After two weeks, she knew that every afternoon Nelson Flowers raised the office blinds and stared out at the street while the building emptied. But since he made her every bit as nervous as he had the first day she'd blundered into the dark office, she generally ducked her head and sped past.

That afternoon, however, determined to act grown up, she restrained her impulse to flee when she reached the bottom of the stairs.

But she'd barely reached the office door when he turned around.

"Yes, Miss O'Brien?"

In her enthusiasm over Vivian's sketch, she'd forgotten to rehearse what she was going to say.

But since she'd already caught his attention, she swallowed hard, flung herself into the office, and spread the drawing over the papers on his desk. "I wanted you to see this."

She was afraid to be caught looking at his scar, so she looked down at the drawing as she held the paper corners and he came to the desk.

He studied the crayon portrait for a long time.

"*Tres vertueux,*" he said at last.

"Vivian Green did it."

He nodded. Then he glanced up. "And—?"

"And I thought—" She swallowed again and took her hands away to let the paper curl. "I wondered if there's a way to encourage her. I think she's very talented."

"I understand you're allowing them drawing time on Fridays."

She refused to defend that hour, and she elevated her chin.

He studied her a moment with his three eyes before he said, "That's probably enough encouragement."

"But for a little girl to do something this good, I thought—"

"I know what you thought. But while rocking the boat is all right occasionally, you don't want to founder it."

She kept her chin raised.

He gave a semi-sigh. "Do you know where the child comes from?"

She shook her head.

"Her Aunt Lily works in the red-light district."

She continued to look at him, and he said, "I try to remember you're not from the South, Miss O'Brien—"

"I never considered Oklahoma the South."

The impertinent contradiction fell from her mouth before she could stop it, and she felt the heat rush to her face as she amended quickly, "I mean, I never thought of Tulsa as a southern town until I got here."

He gave a rueful dip of his head. "I suppose Oklahoma doesn't look like the South to the rest of the nation," he conceded. "Unfortunately, it's a state with the mindset of the Old Confederacy. And those southern attitudes lock *les enfants* of Greenwood into roles of the past. Despite your assessment of little Vivian Green's talent, Miss O'Brien, you need to remember that her aunt's a prostitute."

She'd already mouthed off, and she might as well go for a goat as a sheep, so she said stubbornly, "It shouldn't matter what her aunt is. Vivian should be an artist."

"That may be. But as you and I know, Miss O'Brien— since we are technically now in the South—" He rolled Vivian's portrait up neatly as his sarcasm resurfaced like a bubble of tar. "Here, the most the child can hope to become is a domestic."

She took the sketch of Sam and left the school, clutching the blue portrait and not looking back in case Nelson Flowers' extra eye gazed after her.

After a few blocks she overtook Vivian Green.

"I'm taking your picture home with me." She brandished the scroll. "Do you usually walk to your house down Cincinnati Street?"

"My Aunt Lily got company this afternoon."

"Oh." She didn't want to pursue that subject, and she turned to nod quickly at the red brick mansion they were passing. "That's nice, isn't it?"

Flanked by oaks, the house had a wrap-around verandah and a luxuriant lawn beginning to ripen into the color of wheat. Red geraniums bloomed in urns along the porch, and a black Norwalk, like the automobile Mac drove, stood in the driveway.

Vivian bobbed her little head covered with the stiff black braids that thinned her emaciated neck. "When I grow up, I want me a place like Mr. Flowers."

"That's Mr. Flowers' house?"

Berneen looked closer.

Someone had uprooted every dandelion from the drying grass, had recently washed the car, and had applied fresh paint to the porch railings. The upstairs blinds hugged the windowsills—just as the paper blinds in the school office remained drawn all day—but none of that revealed anything about Nelson Flowers.

"I want red posies for my porch, too."

"Geraniums."

Vivian nodded, and they walked to the end of the block before she said softly, "You know that story about the orphan boy, Miss O'Brien? Do they still educate orphans in England like that Pip?"

"Of course, orphans can be educated. In England or anywhere else. Just because they don't have parents doesn't mean they aren't smart. They may have to work harder than children with all the privileges, but there's nothing they can't learn."

Even as she stoutly asserted that, she heard her uncle's contempt for the poor overlapping Nelson Flowers' prediction that Vivian was doomed to servitude, and she glanced away from the little girl's tiny smile as they started toward a hill with a stand of elms.

Vivian Green maintained a thoughtful silence for another block before she asked, "Do books you read ever tell about girls?"

"Of course they do. In fact, one of my favorite novels, *Jane Eyre,* is about a little girl who grows up in an orphanage. I think you'd like it. You can go to the fiction shelves in the library and look for Charlotte Bronte. Or you can ask the librarian for help. Tell her I said you wouldn't have any trouble reading a Victorian novel."

The shake of her little head and the sober little smile took on a touch of pity. "Our library ain't got fiction books, Miss O'Brien. Or a librarian."

"Not the library beside Mrs. Johnson's rooming house. I meant the big library, the Carnegie Library on Fifteenth Street."

The smile vanished and the shadows under Vivian's eyes deepened. "You ain't from here. But you listen to me. Don't you get yourself in trouble by walking into no library for white people."

SEVEN
....

Had she heard Vivian right?

Had the little girl actually thought she was black?

She turned onto Peoria and glanced down at her bare arms.

Her skin, sun-mottled under the trees, probably did—as her mother would have bemoaned—"look browner than a berry." Her mother had refused to let her have pierced ears—"You look enough like a wild Shoshone as it is," and Berneen guessed she wouldn't have been all that surprised by the error.

She found herself approaching her uncle's twin junipers.

Of course, if she had been black, she certainly couldn't have walked between his cedars chopped into those precarious green balls. She couldn't have gone onto his front porch.

No matter where Ivory lived in Langston, even if her house rivaled the mansion Nelson Flowers owned in

Greenwood, when she arrived in uptown Tulsa, she had to walk down the alley, through the picket gate to the back.

Just like the deliveryman who lugged in the blocks of ice for the icebox and the gardener who mowed the lawn and squared the stiff leaves of the hedges, Ivory had to cross the driveway and enter the house by the kitchen.

Berneen knew that if she really had been black, she could never have gone up the front steps or have put a hand on the burnished knob of the front door unless she did it with a rag and a tin of brass polish.

She sighed as she went inside.

Since she couldn't mention Vivian Green or her innocent mistake over the weekend, Berneen waited impatiently for Monday, eager to tell Caroline.

Every weekday morning, Caroline's resplendent necklace and penciled eyebrows would be waiting, and in the two weeks she'd been at Liberty Elementary, Berneen found a companionship she'd never had before. She'd never had a best friend—or for that matter even a girl her age in town after Phyllis Peterson died of diphtheria when they were ten—and she hadn't learned how to relate to her college classmates, who had come to the school with their alliances already formed. Her mother had always told her everything, but that wasn't like having a best friend to confide in.

That Monday morning she was later than usual getting to school, however, and Caroline wasn't out front.

Berneen drew a disappointed breath as she went inside and clicked down the hall to Persephone's classroom.

She stopped on the threshold.

Nelson Flowers leaned against the window ledge with his arms crossed over his chest, Caroline perched on the children's table, her elbows resting on her knees, and

Persephone sat at her desk. Gray-haired Hanford Yarborough, standing before the first row of little desks, had evidently just started reading aloud from the front page of the *Tulsa Tribune*.

Berneen knew at once she couldn't bring up Vivian Green—or her charming error—in the presence of all four of them.

Caroline waved a ringed hand, and commanded, "Oh, Hanford, here's Berneen. Start over."

Everyone stared as she came through the door, and she felt blood rush to her face.

"I don't know why Miss O'Brien needs to hear it. It's hardly educational," Hanford Yarborough objected peevishly. He had shaggy gray brows that connected straight across his nose, and he always seemed to be peering sadly from under an immobile gray caterpillar. "It concerns Wobblies. I don't see why Miss O'Brien needs to know anything about the Wobblies."

Berneen sat down on the nearest small desktop and opened her mouth to tell Hanford Yarborough she already knew about the Wobblies. But before she'd steadied herself in the embarrassment of being the sudden center of attention, Nelson Flowers said, "Miss O'Brien isn't from the South. It wouldn't hurt for her to know what's going on here in Tulsa."

The morning light made his scar tissue glitter with the sheen of satin.

Hanford Yarborough produced a resigned shrug that bobbed both his celluloid collar and his eyebrow. "Very well."

He cleared his throat and began to read in his church-deacon's monotone. "'We don't have time for mistakes. We have to guard against labor agitators who want to destroy America. If the Wobblies get busy in your neighborhood, kindly take occasion to decrease the supply of hemp in the stores. Knowledge of how to tie a knot might also come in handy. This is no time to waste money on trials. All that is necessary is the evidence and a firing squad. We need to kill Wobblies as we would any other kind of snake.'"

He raised the gray swatch of rug. "That's from an editorial on the front page, Miss O'Brien."

"It was written by a member of the Ku Klux Klan," Nelson Flowers explained.

She knew more about the Klan than she did about Wobblies since she'd read stories in *The Denver Post* about the beatings and whippings and lynchings the Klan used to terrorize minorities and people they didn't like.

But before she could say that either, Hanford Yarborough added, "We don't need to worry about the Klan here, Miss O'Brien. If we don't get involved with people like the Wobblies, we can avoid notice by the Klan. No one will bother us in Greenwood as long as we mind our own business."

"That may be burying your head too deep in the sand, Hanford. Thousands of men in Tulsa belong to the Klan." Nelson Flowers slid a glance at Berneen. "Remember this is still the South."

"If we live and let live, we won't alienate anyone," Hanford Yarborough insisted primly.

"My daddy says every city official in Tulsa is in the Klan," Caroline said. "I'll give y'all odds even Sheriff McCoy belongs."

Nelson Flowers uncrossed his arms and straightened from the windowsill. "The Klan's as strong here as it is anywhere. But let's hope you're right, Hanford. Let's hope Greenwood can steer clear of both Klansmen and white mobs."

Berneen tried not to wince at the way he said, "white."

Caroline turned to her. "You haven't run into anything like this before, have you, Berneen, being from Wyoming and all? But here you need to watch out. No one ever knows when a Klansman will get a bee in his bonnet and trouble will start."

Something about her counsel set off a faint warning at the base of Berneen's skull.

"Now, Caroline, there's no need to frighten Berneen." Persephone said. "We may have the Klan here, but we don't have many fanatics like that one in the paper."

Nelson Flowers turned his intense eyes and scar toward Berneen. "At any rate, it's best not to rock too many boats."

"And just don't let the white people in Tulsa get to you, girl," Caroline finished brightly.

Berneen sat frozen on the little desktop.

She knew what Caroline was thinking.

She knew what all of them were thinking.

She was sure the throbbing vein in her forehead had to be visible—and audible in its pounding—while she sat and they talked around her.

They'd concluded what little Vivian Green had concluded.

She didn't know how many seconds—or minutes—passed before the bell on the playground began its ear-splitting resonance.

The child bell-ringer vigorously prolonged his duty until Nelson Flowers shook his head, murmured something in French, and hurried out.

Everyone else filed from Persephone's room as the bell stopped.

Berneen staggered up the stairs with Caroline, but she couldn't untangle a word of what Caroline was saying as they climbed to the second floor and separated into their classrooms.

In all good faith, they'd accepted her.

But how would they react if she informed them she was white?

Wouldn't they all agree with what she'd thought initially —that she shouldn't have taken the job?

The way she'd always let her mother do the talking, she let Caroline dominate conversations. She wedged a few things about herself into Caroline's monologues, and then she'd more or less let Caroline make up what she wanted from the fragments.

But it never occurred to her that Caroline would make that up.

During the morning, she managed to concentrate long enough to read aloud a chapter of *Great Expectations*. But by the time she picked up the history book, she couldn't make heads or tails of a single paragraph.

Fortunately, a downpour began at lunchtime, and by mid-afternoon, she couldn't be heard over the pounding rain. She let the children sit at their desks, practice multi-plication tables, and whisper among themselves.

She stared out the window.

Finally a fourth grader raced through the rain to pull the bell rope, and Berneen turned to watch the children put away their tablets, take off their shoes, and stuff socks into their pockets.

"Bye, Miss O'Brien."

As soon as they disappeared, she hurried downstairs and rushed outside.

In an instant, her dress and stockings were soaked, and she realized that she, too, should have removed her shoes. But it was too late by then, and as her marcelled waves washed straight, she ducked her head and ran.

She reached the railroad tracks that separated Deep Greenwood from white Tulsa and stepped gingerly over the glistening railroad ties. Water bubbled in the ditches beside the rails, but her shoes were already sodden, so she splashed straight through the ankle-deep puddles.

Wouldn't everyone at school be happier if she didn't say anything?

She'd had no intention of pretending or of passing herself off as something she wasn't when she accepted the job. In fact, she'd congratulated herself for overcoming prejudice, for fitting in so well that her colleagues and the people of Greenwood overlooked her race.

But her whole premise had been false.

They'd simply thought all along she was black.

She made it to First Street and dodged through curtains of water from one awning to the next until she reached the Drexel Building.

The Drexel's shoeshine stand was sheltered from the rain by a glass marquee, and the young bootblack she saw every day outside the building was bending over the shoes of a paunchy white man.

The shoeshine boy seemed about her age, but he never glanced up. Even in early mornings when the two of them were the only people on the street, he never looked up. Once or twice she'd thought about speaking to the top of his lowered head, but after walking by in silence for a couple of weeks, she'd have felt ridiculous abruptly blurting out "Hello," so she'd never greeted him.

He didn't look at her this time either as she hugged the side of the building and passed his stand, but she could feel the white man staring.

And abruptly, she knew in the geography of the moment, that if she were walking on Archer, the boy would look at her appreciatively, just the way the big-stomached white man was watching her.

Across the tracks in Greenwood, the young man could safely stare at her legs.

It was merely a matter of place.

EIGHT

She curled up in the loft, hearing water batter the fan-shaped window, hearing branches scrape the bricks of the garage like clawing animals.

Wasn't this one of those times she should just keep quiet?

Wasn't this the perfect opportunity not to rock the boat?

Sleep was out of the question, and she listened to the rain while she stared at the dark slant of the wall on which she'd thumbtacked the sketch of Sam Rollins.

If she kept quiet about what she now knew everyone believed, if she didn't say anything to Nelson Flowers or to Caroline or Persephone, she might be found out eventually.

That was simple.

But if she went to the office the next day and corrected their error, she'd be found out at once.

That was even simpler.

About midnight, she threw back the quilts and climbed out of bed.

The floor felt cold and damp, but she didn't step into the carpet slippers as she snapped on the light and took her mother's beaver coat from the armoire.

She thrust her arms through the satin-lined sleeves, fastened the fur-covered buttons, and studied herself in the armoire mirror.

She'd never before fully realized what the term "black Irish" implied, but now she did.

She *was* dark.

Her eyes were dark, and even though her dark hair didn't have the texture the children teased each other about, its glassy crimping did appear the same as the pressed, straightened, and curled waves of women she passed all the time on Archer Avenue.

She buried her chin in the fur collar.

She'd seen a beaver coat almost identical to it displayed in the window of Elliott's and Hooker's Dry Goods Store on North Greenwood, so she knew it wasn't a coat only white women wore.

She could say honestly the fur had belonged to her mother, and the truth wouldn't necessarily give her away.

As soon as that conclusion scudded through her head, she clamped her teeth over her lower lip and took off the coat.

Even without knowing she was going to, she'd resolved to pretend.

The next morning she rode the trolley, but when she climbed down at Greenwood and crossed the tracks, she felt as if she'd run all the way from uptown.

That morning, Caroline waited at the front door. "Didn't

you just about drown in that flood yesterday?" Her hand mimicked cascading water, and the rings glittered. "I figured we'd be candidates for pneumonia, so I brought us some sumac tea this morning. I bet that's something you didn't have in Wyoming, did you? My Aunt Belle insists it's better than chicken soup for what ails you."

As she gestured her ring-bound hands and talked with her usual non-stop eagerness, Berneen couldn't see any change in her.

But she knew *she* was different. Now she was allowing the deception.

It dawned on her that since she always arrived at school from the direction of First Street and Archer Avenue, Caroline must suppose she lived in a servant's quarters uptown. But she'd never asked, and Berneen realized—also for the first time—that people in Greenwood probably avoided prying into what jobs one did in white households in exchange for lodging or what kind of white employer one lived with.

As Caroline hurried them down the hall—with her usual clinking of silver—Berneen felt a strange "halving" sensation.

While she walked beside Caroline, she also hovered overhead and saw herself walking along the waxed floor to face Persephone.

When they came in, Persephone smiled, showing her gold crowns and one white tooth, while she busily set out three teacups.

Caroline deftly poured honey-colored liquid from a Mason jar into the cups. "Now, y'all taste that and tell me what you think. It's Indian lemonade." She handed them each a cup. "My Aunt Belle boils up gallons of it all summer.

Would you believe? Persephone's lived here all her life, and she's never tasted it either."

The lukewarm liquid had a woody flavor and swirls of what might have been bark or crushed seeds in the bottom of the cup.

Berneen murmured, "M-m-m-m," while Persephone said, "I reckon it better be good for you."

"It's made from boiling the berries of the sumac tree. Not the poison white berries, but the red sumac, so y'all don't have to worry. It's a recipe handed down from my Cherokee ancestors."

Persephone gave Berneen her conspirator's wink. "I swear, Caroline Mankiller, I don't know what you'd do if you couldn't bring up those Cherokee ancestors of yours with every other breath."

Caroline grinned, not in the least offended. "Well, you have to admit the Mankillers were fascinating characters. They owned big cotton plantations and scores of slaves. Would you believe? Great-granddaddy fought to *save* the Confederacy!"

Persephone shook her head as she smiled. "Enough freedmen lived in Indian Territory after the Civil War to make people think Oklahoma might become the first black state in the nation."

Berneen had realized within the first week of school that Caroline and Persephone considered her Wyoming oil town the end of the earth and that they enjoyed educating her in the ways of the South. Now, of course, she also realized part of what they enjoyed was teaching the innocent northern Negro girl they'd accepted she was.

"Wouldn't a Negro state have been a hoot?" Caroline shouted cheerfully as the racket of the bell began.

Persephone stacked the cups, and Caroline recapped the Mason jar.

Berneen watched them and told herself they had all behaved quite the same as the previous week.

Then, as she and Caroline went into the hall, she abruptly realized that part of her uncle's problem with "darkies" was his fear that in Oklahoma *he* could become the minority.

NINE
●●●●●●●●●●

"Miss O'Brien, you want me to peel off September? It's good and gone." Sam Rollins' long fingers tapped the undertaker's free calendar.

"I get October." Beata Jackson dibbed quickly.

Berneen hadn't seen any alteration in the children's behavior from the opening day of school, and she assured herself that September had proceeded exactly like the first two weeks when she'd thought they all knew she was white.

But even as she monitored her actions and carefully avoided anything that could indicate her race, she wondered with dread how long it would be before someone discovered her secret.

October winds swept into the Magic City with gale force, and for the first time since Berneen had come to her uncle's house, Ivory left for a visit to Langston.

Berneen knew by then that Langston was an all-Negro town, nearly five hours away by bus, and as much as she hated to admit it, she breathed easier knowing that Ivory's husband and two teen-aged sons lived far from Tulsa and that Ivory rarely—if ever—ventured across the tracks. Once Ivory had mentioned the Williams' Dreamland Theatre on Archer and had murmured wistfully, "I wouldn't mind seeing a show once in a while, but them boys need new shoes every time I turn around."

Berneen hadn't said anything, but she felt combined twinges of guilt and relief that after all that time of working for her uncle, Ivory still hadn't become acquainted with the people of Greenwood.

Ivory intended to stay in Langston for a week, and before she returned, the winds turned icy. They blustered around the yellow bricks of downtown buildings and rattled the windows of Liberty Elementary. The old gardener, who was also the janitor, stoked the furnace in the cellar to warm the rooms for the children who came to school with cracking lips and mittenless fingers. Nelson Flowers began to turn the first graders out onto the playground more often for rousing games of tag to warm them up.

Berneen took her mother's coat from the armoire. She pressed a fur cuff against her cheek as she went down the stairs and out the back gate. When she got on the trolley, she, as usual, stood in the aisle to let herself be pushed further from the front when more passengers joined the bundled office workers and store clerks. She always told herself the crowd made it impossible not to move toward the back, but she also knew that if she ran into anyone from Greenwood, she'd technically be standing in the rear of the trolley.

"Greenwood coming up."

She exited down the back steps.

Caroline apparently saw her—and the coat—coming from half a block away. She held the door open, letting the old janitor's heat escape. "Oh, look at that fur!" She stroked a sleeve as they went inside. "Persephone, look at this! Isn't it just gorgeous! Where did you get it, Berneen? Can I try it on?"

Berneen obediently slid the coat off, and Caroline shrugged it on. She swept grandly between the desks to the far end of the room. "Oh, I know I'll never be able to take it off again, Berneen." She twirled like the doll atop a music box. "Why don't we trade coats? I've got that perfectly good red wool over there." She sashayed back up the aisle between the desks just as Nelson Flowers abruptly appeared in the doorway.

He hadn't made a sound, and the three of them started.

He surveyed them with his ironic glance. "I hope I won't interrupt the fashion show if I point out that today is *le jour de paie*. But perhaps you don't need your pay, Miss Mankiller. You seem well prepared for winter with a beaver fur."

"I'll never in a hundred years be able to afford anything like this," she cried at once. "It's Berneen's. I just put it on for a second so I could see what I'll be missing forever."

He turned toward Berneen, and she felt the electricity of his attention.

"The coat was my mother's." She'd practiced saying it in her head, but somehow it still rang false.

Nelson Flowers made one of his French-laced remarks while he reached in his jacket pocket and dealt out three envelopes.

Berneen felt embarrassment throb into her face as she took her packet of bills and coins. She hadn't been able to tell if his remark had been mocking or not. Or if it had been aimed at her or not.

She glanced at Caroline and Persephone, as she started

to tear off the end of the envelope. But since neither of them immediately opened the sealed flaps of theirs, she couldn't bring herself to look at her first month's pay either.

Caroline swung the hem of the coat. "*Merci.*"

A spur of envy jabbed through the chagrin into Berneen's chest. Why hadn't she thought to say "thank you" in French? Or even in English? Why did she always end up floundering in a stupid silence?

Now she'd sound like a ninny if she said anything at all.

TEN

Berneen watched what she said to the children, to Caroline and Persephone. She made a conscious effort to buy everything she needed in Greenwood, and she continued to stand in the back of the trolley, mornings and afternoons.

But by the end of October, she'd begun to neglect her relentless vigilance, and sometimes—even for two or three days at a time—she forgot that she had a secret and a double life and behaved as she would have behaved anywhere.

On Halloween, Mount Zion Baptist Church took up another collection for school books, and Caroline—who knew everybody's business—told Persephone and Berneen that the minister had handed Deacon Hanford Yarborough the handsome sum of sixteen dollars. "Mr. Flowers says it's enough to buy books for the first and second graders."

Even though Caroline could relax and banter with him, she never called Nelson Flowers by his first name in the casual way she did everyone else.

"We'll be able to keep the littlest pests busy for the rest of the year at any rate." Then she added in rapid non sequitur, "Why don't we all go down to Cain's after school and celebrate?"

"Caroline Mankiller, you know Cain's choc shop is no place for a married woman who has dinner to fix," Persephone scolded. "And you know Berneen's too young to get in the door."

"She'll be with me. They'll let her in." Caroline said gaily. "You haven't been to a choc joint, have you, Berneen? I bet you don't have them in Wyoming, do you?"

"The 'choc' isn't chocolate milk but Choctaw beer," Persephone explained. "And the business is more a speakeasy than a confectionary."

If they'd had the conversation during the first two weeks of school, Berneen might have said she had been to a speakeasy once. But now, since she didn't know if speakeasies were frequented only by white people, she didn't confess she knew anything about them.

"Don't worry, Persephone," Caroline went on. "I won't let Berneen have any Choctaw beer. My daddy'd kill me if he heard I was a bad influence on such an innocent."

A spitting of snow dusted the sidewalk as they left school that afternoon, and a light sleet started before they'd gone a block.

Berneen struggled to hold the flaps of the fur coat together, but Caroline managed to keep up a running conversation as the wind swirled empty cigarette packets around them and flung tiny ice chips against their cheeks.

"My daddy's handling the sale of the Red Wing Café there." She pointed. "You wouldn't believe how much Lewis

Reynolds is willing to pay for it. But then, Lewis wants to join a brown-bag club so bad, he'd do anything to get an invitation."

That was Berneen's cue, and she asked dutifully into the sleet, "What's a brown-bag club?"

"It's for the upper crust, the elite. At the dances, hostesses tack a grocery bag up beside the door, and every guest has to put a hand on the brown bag. Anyone whose hand is the color of brown paper can come in. Anyone who's not light enough has got to go dance at some low-down place like Cain's."

She gave Berneen a sly grin as she halted at a narrow storefront with a solid wooden door. "CAIN'S" had been painted in blue enamel on the lintel.

"You wouldn't have any trouble getting into a brown-bag club or into a blue-vein society ball." She lifted Berneen's wrist and tapped the vein that showed blue under the skin. "But wait until you see how much more fun it is to dance at Cain's."

She knocked with a confident rap.

A little shuttered window in the door cracked a narrow slit, and an eye stared out.

Caroline gazed back at the eye and nonchalantly flicked ice motes from her pompadour.

The grate opened, and a battered face filled the square. A diagonal knife scar ran from forehead to jaw across a nose—so badly crushed it was no longer recognizable as a nose—and separated the lips into four parts.

The man looked not only damaged but dangerous, and Berneen almost wished he would challenge her age and tell them to go away.

He didn't.

He merely stared out another second, closed the shutter, and unlatched the door.

It swung back enough for a great paw of a hand to gesture them inside.

The forlorn face with its topaz eyes hulked above them, but Caroline said cheerfully, "I brought a friend, Augustus," as she took Berneen's arm and strode into what could have been a hot, densely packed cellar.

If any windows ever existed, they'd been tar-papered over, and when the man shut the door again, cave darkness smothered the room. The only illumination filtered from one bulb under an oiled-paper shade. Cigarette smoke coiled in thick, sluggish ribbons through the darkness. The temperature must have hovered around a hundred degrees.

A gramophone blared ragtime—turned up full volume—into the cavern's air.

Caroline found a tiny iron table with two empty chairs, and as they shed their coats and the record ended, she signaled. "Two Cokes, Augustus!"

Almost immediately Augustus' shadowy, mangled lips grinned from the darkness, and he set two glasses of Coke on the tabletop before he went to the end of the narrow room, rewound the gramophone, and put on another loud jazz tune.

Caroline sipped the Coke, then leaned across the little table. "Oh, Lord love a duck! There's Diamond Dick Rollins."

She indicated some vague shapes at the bar, and Berneen peered hard to distinguish a man wearing a topcoat and a fedora.

After a few seconds her eyes adjusted to the dim light, and she could see the little area that served as a dance floor.

She could also see that the young man Caroline had pointed out was sauntering toward them.

He stopped at the edge of the table.

He'd taken off his overcoat, but he'd left on the hat, and he looked down at Caroline from under the jaunty brim while he jerked his head toward the dance floor.

Berneen recognized the young bootblack from the Drexel Building.

Up close, he was an older, deeper bronze, version of Sam Rollins.

He turned away without saying a word, and Caroline got up and followed him. "Be right back, Berneen."

They reached the tiny open space and didn't look at each other while they cocked their heads to absorb the rhythm. Then, in exact time and at the same moment, they sprang into the frantic beat. They didn't touch each other, and neither seemed to lead or follow as they gyrated in perfect unison. Their rapid synchronized steps barely grazed the floor, and it was as if they formed the back and front of the same vibrating coin. Caroline's necklace jounced, her silver ear hoops reflected lunging sparks of yellow light, and her hem twinkled at her ankles. Diamond Dick's trouser legs whipped faster and faster—as if his feet had multiplied—and his elbows pumped like graceful wings. But his hat stayed firmly anchored.

Berneen couldn't breathe around the heat and the wild movement on the little postage stamp of floor. Then the gramophone began to run down.

Caroline and Diamond Dick slowed to the increasingly sluggish turns of the record. Their feet became weighted as they, too, wound down and danced slower, slower in the darkness, dual puppets attached to the strings of a nodding puppeteer. Their movements coincided flawlessly, and when the turntable stopped, they halted at a tilt, dead in their tracks.

Everyone stared for a breathless second before they began to applaud. Men whooped and whistled, women clapped and shouted.

Augustus didn't rewind the record player this time, and Caroline and Diamond Dick came to life. They bowed together and separated.

The bootblack melted into the darkness, and Caroline slid into her chair.

"Isn't Diamond Dick fabulous? He's way too dark to be allowed in a brown-bag club dance, but those high-yeller gals, whose mamas won't let them associate with riff-raff, would give their eyeteeth to whirl around the floor with him." She wiped her sweat-beaded forehead. "Oh, look who just came in."

Her too-loud whisper sailed across a momentary silence, and when Berneen glanced over to see Nelson Flowers at the end of the bar, she was sure he'd heard. Blood rushed to her head again and her breath stopped.

He nodded at them before he turned to talk to the man beside him.

Berneen slid her gaze back to the Coke glass in her hand, but she found herself wondering if Nelson Flowers, who could never pass a brown-bag or a blue-vein test either, could dance as well as Diamond Dick.

ELEVEN

························

Berneen decided after barely a month that her uncle had jelled in suspended animation.

Even though wintry weather crisped his lawn, dropped the leaves of his sycamores to the driveway like scattered gold coins, and shriveled his American Beauties on their bushes, he didn't alter. He continued to dress in a series of identical shirts and pin-striped suits, his face kept its sunburn, and although his candidate, Harding, was elected president in November, her uncle maintained his preoccupation with trench warfare and the battle in the Argonne Forest where he'd been wounded in the leg.

He never asked if Berneen liked Tulsa or what she did with her spare time. He didn't seem to know—or care—when she went with Caroline to the Dreamland. He never asked where she'd been after she returned from Williams' Confectionary where she and Caroline ate sundaes that Caroline insisted were to die for. Her uncle always informed her when he was going to one of his meetings, which she could tell were important to him, but since he didn't appear to have any other social life, she was surprised one evening when he announced brusquely, "The head of the legal department throws a party every December. It's a yearly *de rigueur* affair on the first day of the month."

Berneen was sure Nelson Flowers would have pronounced the French with a better accent.

Then her uncle dumbfounded her further by taking out his wallet and laying some stiff greenbacks on the tablecloth. "I don't know if you brought evening clothes. You might see something you like at Lesterman's."

He gently knuckled the top of Black Jack Pershing's head, put the cat down, and left the dining room.

Berneen stared at the bills tucked under her uncle's serving plate.

Had that been his way of inviting her to the party?

She sighed.

She probably did owe him some gratitude for the months of free rent, and if he wanted her to attend a stiff company party, she could put up with the discomfort for an evening.

But she couldn't go to Lesterman's for a party dress.

She took up the money and heard as clearly as if Vivian Green stood in her uncle's dining room, the little gir's caution about going into a white store.

She and Caroline had passed Elliott's and Hooker's and had seen a shift incrusted with cut jet beads, so she stopped there the next day after school.

"That be some fine outfit," the salesgirl admired happily when she paired the dress to matching patent leather pumps.

She had no idea what time the party might be—or even

if she'd actually been invited—but on the first of December, right after dinner, she dressed in her fine outfit, sat down on the bed—being careful not to snag the jet facets on the chenille—and waited.

Within an hour, Ivory knocked at the door. "Miss, your uncle says he called the taxi. He don't like to drive in the snow."

"Thank you, Ivory."

She grabbed the beaver coat and followed Ivory down the stairs as a car horn sounded out front.

"I'm glad you're ready," her uncle said shortly.

It was his most arrogant tone, and for a second she considered informing him coldly he could go to his stupid party alone.

But he looked so awkward and uncomfortable in a tuxedo that she felt sorry for him, and she hesitated just long enough for the taxi to honk again.

Her uncle ushered her out the front door.

He gave the taxi driver an address, and, in no time, they arrived at a huge house of antique brick with massive columns and a lawn that could have supported a dozen thoroughbreds.

Hordes of people milled behind the lighted, polished windows.

Her uncle paid the cabby and took her elbow as they walked up the snow-shoveled walk.

He rang the doorbell, and a woman opened the door and made a fake "Glad-you-could-come" speech. She was resplendent in ecru ostrich feathers and chiffon, topped off by a diamond tiara and a diamond necklace nearly as gaudy as Caroline's silver squash blossom. Her uncle introduced Berneen, and after a ritual handshake with the woman and a man who was probably the host, Berneen and her uncle stepped down into an oyster-colored living room overflowing with Waterford punch bowls, hot-house lilies in crystal vases, silver trays of hors d'oeuvres, and scores of people.

The men wore tuxedos with boiled shirts, and although some women probably weren't dressed in milky organza, all of them were so awash in diamonds and pearls they seemed as pallid as the snow outside.

The party was every bit as bad as she'd anticipated.

After only a few minutes, however, she recognized that what discomfited her most wasn't that she was the youngest one in the room or that she had nothing in common with anyone there, but that everyone around her looked alike. They all seemed to have blond hair, transparent eyebrows, the kind of blue-white complexions her mother called "wormy," and they radiated about as much vitality as the bathtub gin in their glasses.

For the past three months, she'd lived with color. She'd become accustomed to red brick buildings and red brick sidewalks, to bright enamels, to companions with brilliance and animation in their very pigment. And now as she plastered on a smile and dutifully followed her uncle, she admitted to the startling conclusion that after only three months in Greenwood, she no longer fit in a white world.

She'd stopped identifying herself as white.

But she also knew that no matter how dark her tan might get, no matter how often she forgot about race when she walked on Archer Avenue, she wasn't black either.

TWELVE
....

The second week in December, Nelson Flowers carried a huge spruce tree into the school on his shoulder, and the old janitor affixed it to a stand at the foot of the stairs.

Berneen bought red and green construction paper and had Ivory mix up a huge jar of flour-and-water paste so all the children—even the first graders—could make paper chains. Caroline said she could persuade her father to donate oranges, cloves, and string to fashion pom-poms, and Persephone volunteered to bake gingerbread men to hang from the branches.

Hanford Yarborough avoided what he called "the frivolity of decorating" and instead organized a rummage sale at Mount Zion Church. "It's our Christian duty to give poor parents a chance to buy gifts at bargain prices."

"If you ask me, a rummage sale is a demeaning, Uncle Tom endeavor," Caroline complained after he'd left the room.

"No one's asking you, Caroline," Persephone said, frowning a warning for her to lower her voice.

Caroline paid no attention. "Just wait until you start sorting that donated trash, Berneen. Most of the bric-a-brac will be chipped, and most of the clothes will reek of perspiration. You won't believe the garbage we get from uptown."

Her words carried far down the hall as usual, and Hanford Yarborough's solemn footsteps backtracked to the doorway.

His gray eyebrow bristled. "It doesn't hurt to give thanks for what we receive, Miss Mankiller."

Caroline, as was her morning habit, sat on the children's table with her hands clasped around the long skirt. "Sometimes I think you put too much stock in the fact that the mealymouthed will inherit the earth, Hanford."

"Now, Caroline," Persephone soothed and attempted to change the subject. "Did you bring us some news from the paper this morning, Hanford? I told Zacharia you were my source of knowing what's going on in the world."

He refused to be diverted and continued to scowl at Caroline. "Some of us need to learn to be thankful for everything around us," he said. "We must take what the Lord provides and give thanks."

"My daddy heard that vigilantes stormed the Wobbly offices on Fourth Street last night. They took the Wobblies out by the river and tarred and feathered them." She wrinkled her nose and pursed her lips. "Are you saying we're supposed to be thankful for that?"

He studied her with disapproving melancholy, and his gray caterpillar drooped stray hairs over his eyes. "We can be thankful, Miss Mankiller, that it didn't happen in Greenwood."

Berneen had momentarily put aside *Great Expectations* to borrow *The Christmas Carol* from her uncle's study, and the children happily slathered paste on paper strips and linked the circles together while they listened to Scrooge's transformation and redemption.

The building took on scents of pine, orange, and clove, and everyone but Hanford Yarborough brimmed with holiday cheerfulness.

Hanford Yarborough stayed as glum as ever.

He'd apparently been more offended by Caroline than anyone knew. Despite the fact that his church rummage sale went off smoothly, he continued to admonish Caroline— and by extension Berneen and Persephone, who sat in the room with her. He began a blitz of newspaper articles, clipped out daily to prove that virtue stemmed from being thankful and from tending to one's own affairs.

Berneen tried to remember that he had an ailing wife and that his life revolved around Mount Zion Church, but she might have started rolling her eyes every time he appeared if the Christmas holiday hadn't arrived to give them all a reprieve.

For lunch on Christmas Eve Nelson Flowers produced enough bakery rolls for everyone, a wheel of cheese to be sliced into individual triangles with a clasp knife, and a bag of hard candies containing enough pieces for each child to have three. Berneen and Caroline passed out the oranges and gingerbread men, and everyone left the little school so the janitor could lock up for the week.

Caroline had freely discussed the gloves and rhinestone jewelry she'd bought for her parents, siblings, her Aunt Belle and cousin Oralee, but since Berneen's uncle hadn't put up a tree and since Ivory planned to go home to Langston, Berneen resisted the temptation to buy gifts.

Christmas morning, she deliberately slept late, and when she wandered into the empty house, she told herself she was relieved to see that no one had left any packages in the kitchen or in the study for her.

She told herself she was equally glad her uncle would be spending the day at the Petroleum Club.

With Ivory gone, in fact, her uncle spent most of Christmas week away from the house, and Berneen relaxed in the bead-bedecked parlor, cuddling Black Jack Pershing in her lap while she read.

A week of doing nothing but reading Anthony Trollope's novels was enough relaxation, however, and by January 2, she could hardly wait to get back to school and to find out what Caroline had received for Christmas, to hear about the exciting things she'd done with her sisters and her young cousin over the holiday.

Berneen hurried from the trolley stop in a fresh snow whose flakes clumped together and spiraled like wet feathers through the air.

The little school looked welcoming and homey. The snow sparkled unblemished on the narrow stretch of front lawn, and only a few footsteps broke the crust to the front door. Berneen smiled as she planted her new galoshes in the already indented prints.

Slush had tracked a few yards down the hall, and she stamped off her overshoes and undid the buckles, which jingled as she went toward Persephone's room.

Persephone and Hanford Yarborough had arrived before her.

"Good morning, Miss O'Brien."

He already held an open *Tulsa Daily Star*, and he obviously stood poised to read to them.

Berneen caught herself before she sighed.

"Did you have a nice holiday, Berneen?" Persephone asked with kind solicitude.

While she told them she'd had quite a refreshing time, she heard Caroline's hearty step in the hallway.

Almost at once, Caroline appeared in the doorway.

"Miss Mankiller," Hanford Yarborough said solemnly. Then he looked beyond her. "Good morning, Nelson."

Nelson Flowers had walked up behind Caroline without a sound.

"I hope everyone had a satisfactory Noël."

Before anyone could answer, Hanford Yarborough interposed, "I've brought in an article, which I believe every one of you needs to hear."

Caroline gave Berneen a "heaven-help-us" look.

"But I must warn you it is not a pleasant piece."

Berneen could tell there was no way they could avoid the news story—pleasant or not—when Hanford Yarborough began at once.

"This happened in Georgia. Listen to what it says. 'They brought the arrested Negro from the jail. Five hundred men rushed on the armed sheriffs, who made no resistance whatever. They tore the Negro's clothes off before he was placed in a waiting automobile. The Negro was unsexed and made to eat a portion of his anatomy which had been cut away."

Queasiness lodged in Berneen's forehead, and her breath caught somewhere between her nostrils and her lungs.

"'Then the man was taken to a grove, where each one of

more than five hundred people, in a Ku Klux ceremonial, had placed a pine nut around a stump, making a pyramid ten feet high. The Negro was chained to the stump and asked if he had anything to say. Castrated and in indescribable torture, he asked for a cigarette and blew the smoke in the faces of his tormentors. The pyre was lit, and the men and women, old and young, grandmothers among them, joined hands and danced while the Negro burned.'"

Hanford Yarborough stopped reading and began to fold the paper.

Berneen could hear the paper creasing, but she couldn't see clearly through the horrifying images that clung to the back of her eyes.

No one said anything, and only the paper crackled across the little empty desks.

Finally Hanford Yarborough cleared his throat. "As I said, that happened in Georgia. No similar sort of thing will happen here as long as we tend to our own affairs. And as long as we avoid activities that can incite the Klan to—"

Nelson Flowers didn't let him finish. "You're right, Hanford. We won't submit to a lynching here. Too many of us remember why we fought the last war."

"I wasn't referring to a war mentality, Nelson. I meant only that influential people in Tulsa know Archer Avenue is respectable and prosperous. The Wobblies have been sent packing, so the Klan has nothing to worry about from outside agitators."

"Hang the Wobblies! What makes you think the man those *camelotes* lynched in Georgia wasn't prosperous or respectable? What makes you think he didn't know influential people?" The hollow in his cheek rippled with angry striations. "A black man doesn't have to do or be anything to get burned at the stake. Especially if the Klan decides he crossed the dividing line between the races."

The phrase, "crossed the dividing line," ricocheted inside Berneen's head. Nausea collected in her stomach.

She missed Hanford Yarborough's next comment, and she only refocused her attention as Nelson Flowers was concluding, "Too many of us held onto the Lugers we picked up in the war."

Mac had bought a Luger at a pawnshop in Casper, and Berneen knew it was a German army pistol. She looked hard at Nelson Flowers.

"If we have to die, it won't be like dogs," he added fiercely.

Persephone said quickly, "Now, Nelson. There's no use trying to anticipate what the Klan will do or what we'll do."

"There's no need for such firebrand talk, Nelson," Hanford Yarborough seconded. "We've been living side by side with white folks for sixty years. I see no cause not to keep the peace."

Nelson Flowers impatiently pushed up a sleeve to reveal a gold watch, whose gold band intersected a long, deep scar on his wrist. "We got mustered out like men. We're not going to be butchered like hogs."

"Now, Nelson, we need to keep reasonable heads if we're to—"

Nelson Flowers interrupted him with a sentence of biting French and strode out.

Berneen stared after him bewildered.

He'd said, "We got mustered out."

Just as if he'd been in the army.

After a moment, Caroline murmured, in a voice that, for once, approximated a whisper, "My daddy says Mr. Flowers is a bit of a hothead."

"Maybe he's earned the right to be more hotheaded than the rest of us," Persephone said with gentle reproof.

"We wouldn't want someone from the Klan to hear those idle threats."

"Maybe they're not idle, Hanford, considering his war record."

"His war record makes no difference. He could get us all in trouble." Hanford Yarborough finished folding the newspaper.

In the silence Berneen ventured carefully, "I didn't know Mr. Flowers had a war record."

"He was wounded in the Argonne Forest," Persephone said.

Berneen's lips parted in astonishment. He'd been in the Argonne Forest? He'd been in France with her uncle?

THIRTEEN
·················

That night at dinner, she didn't let her uncle start praising President Harding—which he'd done weekly since the election—or begin reminiscing before she said, "I heard today that colored soldiers from Tulsa also fought in France."

"Where did you hear that kind of drivel?"

She didn't answer the "where" since she'd prepared for it, and she repeated, "I didn't know black soldiers from Tulsa had been in France with you."

"That's ridiculous," he said sharply as he took off his pince-nez. "There were *no* colored soldiers in France with me. From Tulsa or anywhere else. Some darkies undoubtedly were allowed to join the army, but colored men weren't soldiers. Wherever they were, in the States or overseas, they served as camp cooks and bootblacks."

"I understood that some colored troops fought," she persisted, "and that some of them were decorated for bravery."

"Nonsense."

"But if they had been in the Argonne Forest—"

"Don't let anyone hear you suggest that Negroes fought in the Argonne. To imply that is an insult to the men who died there." His eyes flashed in the candlelight. "Negro troops in France would mean that I'd have more in common with a darkie soldier than I'd have with a white man who hadn't been there." He was silent a long moment. "I'll grant you some coloreds might have avoided kitchen duty by forming company bands in France. As entertainers, there's no denying they have a natural rhythm."

"And pearly white teeth," she threw in sarcastically.

She'd told herself before she crossed the driveway and went into dinner that she'd retreat if he put up too much resistance, but backing down wasn't as easy as she'd thought, and she heard herself saying, "I don't see any reason why some of the black men from Tulsa couldn't have been soldiers. There have been black soldiers in the army. They fought in the Civil War."

"Colored soldiers were thrown into the fray by the Union generals as cannon fodder. The darkies in uniform were slaughtered by Rebel soldiers the way horses or oxen were slaughtered."

"Union black soldiers carried arms," she reminded him. "I doubt if the pack horses or mules were equipped with guns."

He discounted her irony and adjusted the little glasses on his nose again. "The coloreds ran mindlessly into the Confederate artillery like lemmings running off cliffs into the ocean."

"The Union generals who supplied the rifles obviously believed the Negroes capable of being soldiers." Her tone remained mutinous despite the fact that she was losing ground. "Black troops fought in a lot of battles."

"The Union army was desperate for bodies. Our army in the Great War had plenty of men. Pershing's officers weren't desperate. They knew the coloreds were not only useless but a liability to real soldiers. No officer would have been fool enough to assign weapons to colored troops. Darkies were given pots and pans, not rifles."

His pince-nez swerved from her toward the centerpiece bowl, which now held sprays of cedar and pinecones.

"General Pershing insisted the coloreds be allowed to train, so they learned to march—with broomsticks. They were Black Jack's blind spot. But he was a good general, and he knew that if the darkies were issued weapons, the entire body of white troops would riot. No one in the army wanted that kind of insurrection."

She stared at his profile while doubts began to gather in her mind.

He was so positive.

Could Nelson Flowers have made up his war record?

He probably had volunteered—even her uncle conceded black men joined the army—and he probably went overseas, where he'd learned his impeccable French. But had he really been in a battle?

Had the scar in his cheek resulted from some accident?

And if he did own a Luger, had he, like Mac, picked it up in a pawnshop?

She went to her room feeling dismal, and almost as soon as she went to bed, she fell into a nightmare.

Inside the leaping flames of a monstrous bonfire, a man stood chained to a tree stump. His mouth opened in a scream, but no sound came from his throat as hooded creatures pranced around the fire, holding hands and laughing silently like a scene from a movie.

She woke herself up, shaking.

But the pale moonlight failed to cancel the terrifying images, and she closed her eyes again.

Immediately, Nelson Flowers danced a buck-and-wing across her retina. Enveloped in an apron, he wore a tall, puffy cook's hat and grinned an Uncle Tom smile.

She opened her eyes and reminded herself that even servants and valets in the army wore khaki. They wouldn't wear chef's hats or aprons.

But if Nelson Flowers lied about being a soldier, maybe he'd never even had a uniform.

Her dismay lasted for the next week, and she went to Persephone's room in the mornings, worried that Nelson Flowers might walk in and that she'd see him as the scraping lackey her uncle insisted all black volunteers had been.

But the week passed and he didn't walk in.

Nor did Caroline or Persephone mention him, and when the three of them met before school that week, Caroline expounded on her brother's upcoming June wedding and the sale of the Red Wing Café, an event making tongues wag all along Archer Avenue—which she laughingly called "Black Wall Street"—because of the vast amount of money involved.

"Caroline, I'd hate for you to be broadcasting my money business around town like that," Persephone said. She tried to steer the conversation to Zacharia's garden. "He's putting out jonquil and iris bulbs. They're about the prettiest flowers in creation. Maybe because they're the first blossoms you see in the spring."

Berneen wasn't interested in wedding plans, the Red Wing Café, or in irises, but as much as she wanted to hear about Nelson Flowers, she felt too inhibited to ask. She waited in vain for Caroline or Persephone to bring up his name.

Still, she didn't want to run into him, and at the end of each school day, she averted her eyes from the office door as she left the building.

She managed to avoid encountering Nelson Flowers into the following week, and she'd momentarily stopped thinking about him as Friday came and she watched her sixth graders trace heart patterns onto red construction paper. "If you do a good job of cutting them out, I'll tack the neatest ones in the front hall so everyone can anticipate Valentine's Day."

When she went downstairs, she carried a handful of the cutouts—actually two from each child—and a bristling mound of borrowed thumbtacks.

Just as she reached the foot of the stairs, Nelson Flowers stepped from the first-grade room.

He'd lowered the shades in the classroom to let the children put their heads down and nap at their little desks, and since it wasn't time for him to raise the office blinds, the hallway had darkened to a dim half-light.

"I see you're decorating the walls, Miss O'Brien," he said. "*Tres createur* of you."

Berneen glanced toward him before she could stop herself, and since she knew there was nothing creative involved in tracing and cutting out paper hearts or in tacking them on the wall, she raised her chin defensively.

But then perhaps because her confidence had grown since August—or possibly because her doubts about him had crowded out her hesitation—she said, in the slightly impudent tone with which she might have defied her uncle, "Did you learn your French when you were in France?"

He pulled the classroom door shut behind him before he answered in sarcastic French. *"Oui."*

"Persephone said you went overseas during the war."

"Yes," he said.

She'd used up her defiance, and her courage wasn't up to questioning whether his war record had been fabricated, so she repeated lamely, "Persephone said a lot of Tulsa troops went to France."

"Most of us who volunteered in 1917 ended up overseas."

She stood holding the red paper hearts and thumbtacks, unable to confront him or ask if he'd lied about being in battle. Nor could she frame a question about his wound. But she couldn't stop herself before she asked, "Why on earth would you volunteer?"

The hall was too dark for her to distinguish his expression, but his voice sounded surprised when he said, "There is such a thing as 'patriotism' in this country."

She couldn't think what to say to a remark that sounded so much like her uncle. Her hand with the paper hearts began to perspire. She knew when she got back to her classroom, she'd discover splotches of red dye on her palm.

"There's plenty wrong with it, but don't forget, this is our nation, too, Miss O'Brien."

She had no response to that either, and after a few wordless seconds she turned away to begin tacking up the paper hearts.

She could have been plowing through a great mass of murky Jell-O, however, and although she tried to act as if her knees and elbows weren't hinged, she felt every muscle solidify to bone.

Everyone still remained in the rooms, but the children napped and worked so noiselessly that Nelson Flowers and Berneen might have been alone in the building. He continued to stand at the foot of the stairs, watching her, and Berneen felt herself move ever more clumsily.

She nonetheless forced herself to concentrate on spacing the paper hearts along the wall.

Then Nelson Flowers said, not as if he were explaining but merely remembering, "Pershing was able to get us trained in the States before we went overseas, but even he couldn't get the white troops to accept us as a fighting unit."

She adjusted the final red heart and pierced the center of it with a thumbtack.

She'd foolishly hoped her uncle had been wrong.

But he hadn't been.

There was nothing more for Nelson Flowers to say. He confirmed that black soldiers hadn't fought with white troops. He corroborated her uncle.

Berneen held herself stock still in the dark hallway while disillusionment coated her tongue.

Nelson Flowers had confessed—not knowing he was confessing—that his scar hadn't been earned in a battle. He'd told her—obviously without knowing what he'd admitted—that his army experience consisted of serving stew to the infantry in the trenches or of grooming horses for the cavalry in the fields.

FOURTEEN

Berneen wanted to retreat to her classroom and deal with her disappointment as far away from him as possible, but since he didn't go back to his first graders and didn't walk to the office, she felt constrained to wait at the bottom of the stairs beside him.

She couldn't face the false war wound, however, and she stared at the floor until he spoke again—in a musing sort of voice. "It took a while, but General Pershing finally persuaded the French army to let us join them."

She looked up startled and peered at him through the gloom.

"Black Jack Pershing believed in us all the way. So we had to show him—as well as the French—what we could do. We were issued French uniforms, and we spent the rest of the war under General Foch. Since we volunteered like the very devil for every mission he offered, Foch couldn't understand what was wrong with the Americans. The French were glad to have us on their side. Particularly in the

Argonne and at Saint-Mihiel where they lost over half their force."

"You fought with the *French* army?"

"Didn't I say that in English?"

But since she couldn't risk sounding utterly mindless by asking again if he'd really said that American black soldiers fought with the French army, she murmured instead, "Persephone said you got wounded in the Argonne."

He stared at her a moment, almost as if he were translating her statement in his head, before he nodded grudgingly. "A couple of us took out a machine-gun nest. Jackson didn't make it back. I only lost a few pieces of flesh and bone to German fire, but the French awarded me the *Crois de Guerre* anyway."

His unwilling, yet diffident, admission told her everything.

She instantly accepted—with unreasoning joy and not a shred of doubt—his version over her uncle's.

She knew with unquestioning certainty that Nelson Flowers had been wounded overseas, that he'd kept his captured German Luger when he was mustered out. And she knew with equal certainty that he was prepared to use it.

She stayed late that afternoon, sitting at her desk with great contentment until everyone else left the building.

Nelson Flowers had fought in the Argonne Forest, where he'd earned a medal for bravery, a *Crois de Guerre.*

She watched snowflakes drift onto the playground.

She wouldn't recognize a *Crois de Guerre,* of course. Or a French uniform for that matter. But she was utterly convinced that Nelson Flowers had possessed both. She was also satisfied that the havoc of German bullets showed in his cheekbone, in his wrist.

The sun was setting by the time she left the school and reached the railroad yard, but enough light remained to show that no trains hurtled toward her from the shadows.

Her uncle had been wrong.

As soon as she got home, she'd enlighten him. He needed to be informed that black troops had fought in the battle he thought he remembered so well. Perhaps he should also hear about what veteran Nelson Flowers was doing now.

And perhaps it was a good time for her to tell him she was teaching at Liberty Elementary in Deep Greenwood.

She waited at a trolley stop a few minutes, but when no trolley appeared in the distance, she started walking. Although the air was crisp and snow clouds covered the evening sky, the snowflakes drifted into the most cheerful night she'd ever seen.

Nelson Flowers had earned a medal for bravery in the war.

She smiled to herself as she saw her uncle's house through the lazy spirals of snow and climbed the front steps under the beam of the porch light.

She sailed through the front door, dropped her galoshes by the hall door, and headed for the library, where a light shone over the desk.

"Uncle Quinn?"

No one sat at the desk, and she went quickly back to the hallway, glancing in at the dining room table, which had been set for dinner. Her uncle wasn't waiting in his host's chair, but since it wasn't yet six, she hadn't really expected to find him.

As she retraced her steps into the hall, she saw a band of light from under a door at the top of the stairs.

It came from the room she'd always assumed was her

uncle's bedroom, and she went halfway up the stairs to the little landing. "Uncle Quinn? Are you home?"

There was no answer, and she went to the top of the staircase and knocked on the door. "Uncle Quinn, I have something to tell you."

She thought she heard a voice, and she gave the door a push.

No one was in the bedroom either.

But a cotton robe and a peaked hood lay unfolded across the bed. A Crusader's cross had been stenciled in red on the robe.

The empty flatness of the unbleached muslin—blazoned with its scarlet cross—could have been a flabby skin shed by one of the phantoms in her nightmare, and the holes cut in the hood could have been a mask over a pair of bandaged eyes.

Nelson Flowers insisted the Ku Klux Klan had thousands of members in Tulsa.

Her uncle was one of them.

She stared down at the bed under the electric glare.

But as she shied from the harsh white robe with its harsh red cross, she recognized that she wasn't stunned by the discovery.

She wasn't even surprised.

She'd learned the first week in his house that her uncle sympathized with Klan attitudes. She suspected he could have urged a lynching, could have helped tar and feather the unfortunate Wobblies. She even surmised—not wanting to, and not articulating it—that in Georgia, he'd have joined the crowd watching the castrated Negro burn to death.

The hood, the halberd-shaped cross, mocked, accused her.

She'd tried to file her suspicions away in an unlit compartment of her mind so she could justifiably accept her uncle's free room and board.

But now, with the evidence spread out neatly before her eyes, she could no longer ignore the conjectures she tried to veil.

She backed away from the bed and pulled the door shut as she returned to the hall.

Her uncle stood on the landing.

FIFTEEN

"I wondered where you were," he said.

Berneen grasped the newel post to steady herself while she coldly examined his red face, his conservative glasses, his seemingly harmless stoop.

Any plans for telling him about Nelson Flowers and the Argonne Forest, about Liberty Elementary or Greenwood, had vanished, and she uttered the only sentence left in her head, "You belong to the Ku Klux Klan."

He beckoned as if he hadn't heard. "Come down now. Ivory has dinner ready."

She didn't move. "All those meetings you go to are Klan meetings, aren't they?"

He started down the stairs.

She braced herself against the banister. "How could you be cruel and indifferent enough to join the Klan? How could you be part of an organization that tortures and maims and murders other human beings?"

He glanced back over the top of his pince-nez. "Where do you manage to pick up those ridiculous notions? Belonging to the Klan is like belonging to the Chamber of Commerce or the Elks' Club."

"All her life Mama wanted to be like you and help people. That's why she became a nurse."

He descended to the bottom of the stairs. "The Klan is one of the few organizations in the nation trying to preserve American ideals. When you have more experience with the South, you'll see how necessary the Klan is."

She studied him coldly, silently.

He took off his pince-nez as he looked up at her. "Eileen wouldn't have objected to the Klan if she'd known anything about it. Klansmen are doctors, lawyers, bankers—patriots with concern for all Americans. And that means darkies as well. Coloreds have the minds of children, and children need a firm hand to guide them."

"You're trying to tell me a brutal lynching is merely 'guiding with a firm hand'?"

"No one is lynched without a just cause, Berneen."

As stony-hearted as she felt toward him, she noticed that it was the first time he'd addressed her by name.

"We want to maintain a separation of the races, which is what everyone wants—even the coloreds. They're more comfortable staying with their own kind. People want to associate with others like themselves." He reached the doorway to the dining room. "Wait until you've been here longer. After you have some contact with Negroes, you'll change your mind about the Klan."

He disappeared into the dining room, but rather than joining him, she fled to her loft room.

She closed the door and looked forlornly around.

Staying above the garage, being served the fine dinners, had been effortless—even pleasant much of the time—but now that she knew about her uncle's Klan affiliation, all ease, all pleasure had disappeared.

What would Caroline and Persephone—and particularly Nelson Flowers—say if they found out that she was not only white, but the niece of a Klansman? That she lived in a free room he provided?

It was no longer possible for her to stay.

So the next day she requested that Caroline ask her father about rooms for rent, and after school she bought *The Tulsa Daily Star* to look up apartments in Greenwood.

She'd been back at her uncle's only long enough to realize there were no apartments listed before she heard Ivory's polite knock on the door.

"I know you plan on moving out, miss," Ivory said without preamble as she stepped inside and pulled the door shut after her.

"I have to."

She sat on the bed with her feet tucked under her, and as she looked at Ivory, her spine sagged.

She'd miss the meals, the cornbread, the little extras—the pressing of her dresses and the mending of her hems—that Ivory found time to do for her. She'd miss Ivory's smile and motherly pride over her sons' good grades in their Langston school. She'd miss her uncle's library and the incongruous parlor, even the solemn regard and purr of Black Jack Pershing.

But there was no way around it.

She'd hate herself if she stayed.

Ivory stood watching her. "Your uncle won't want you to go, miss."

Berneen gave an exaggerated sigh to cover her sadness. "He might notice that no one but Black Jack Pershing is listening to him rehash the war over dinner, but otherwise, he won't care a bit."

"Oh, yes, he will, miss. He's changed with you here."

"What did he change from?" she asked more flippantly than she felt.

She couldn't imagine her uncle being anything other than the dour, red-faced man who opened the door to her knock the night she arrived.

"He used to stare for hours at that red window of his. It's a wonder he didn't put a bullet through his head."

Berneen considered a moment. Then, "He doesn't seem the type to commit suicide."

"There ain't necessarily a type, miss."

Berneen sat another second before she shook her head. "I can't see him doing anything that rash."

"My own daddy covered up the signs good, and we didn't see it coming either, but one day at suppertime, he just whipped out his Bowie knife and cut his own throat, right at the kitchen table."

Berneen shivered. "I'm sorry."

Ivory shrugged.

Berneen swung her feet over the side of the bed and slid them into the carpet slippers. "I guess I just don't want to stay around somebody evil."

"You know your uncle ain't evil, miss."

She focused on the blue portrait of Sam Rollins before she sighed again. "No, I suppose he's not really evil. But I don't want to stay around anyone who condones evil either."

"Sometimes people don't recognize evil when they see it."

Berneen looked curiously into Ivory's golden face. "You knew all along he belonged to the Klan, didn't you?"

Ivory nodded.

"And you can forgive him?"

"Sometimes people need educating more than they need forgiving."

Berneen gave her a wry smile. "Uncle Quinn thinks he knows everything already."

"You can let him know that ain't so. But keep in mind, miss, you can't teach him if you ain't around."

SIXTEEN
·················

She told Ivory she'd consider staying, but since at the moment she couldn't face her uncle, she said, "Could you please tell Uncle Quinn I've got a splitting headache?"

"Yes, miss."

Berneen watched her go out.

Ivory had every right to scorn Quinn O'Brien and his bigotry. Yet she was willing to stay and work for him.

On the other hand, where could a black woman get work if she boycotted any employer who might belong to the Klan? If it were true that most professionals in Tulsa were Klansmen, then every family able to afford a cook or a maid or a gardener paid its annual dues to the Klan.

Berneen continued to sit despondently on the bedspread.

What a shame that her uncle had to be such a follower.

In the war he'd fought for what was right. Why did he

have to come home and betray everything decent, just because he got lonely?

Ivory could hypothesize that he didn't know the Klan was as evil as it was, but, of course, she could be forbearing. And she had the excuse of having to work in a white household.

Berneen didn't have either that necessity or the luxury of Ivory's forgiveness. She had no choice but to condemn the Klan. She had to disavow passionately Klan acts Ivory might ignore. Ivory could forgive and be noble, but if Berneen pardoned the beatings and lynchings, she'd merely be a coward.

And she'd despise herself.

As she began to fold the newspaper, she conceded that her alibi for skipping dinner had indeed become a fact.

She indeed had a spike cleaving her brain.

Her headache persisted until the next morning when Caroline met her and reported cheerfully, "Daddy says there's nothing for rent right now. Greenwood's booming, and drummers are down from all over the U.S. I guess you'll have to wait until school is out to find a place."

"I was hoping I could rent something now."

"Daddy says things will settle down by summer." She raised her penciled brows brightly. "You know, I've been thinking we ought to get an apartment together in the fall."

"That'd be great!" She looked closely at Caroline. "But would you really be willing to move away from home?"

"I'll give you odds Daddy finds us a place down the street from our house. Somewhere like Grace Johnson's rooms." She grinned. "You'd have to eat Aunt Belle's fried chicken or my mama's greens once a week though."

As the school bell clamored and they separated into their

rooms, Berneen decided that she'd room with Caroline in the fall.

She'd become a part of Greenwood full time.

And her secret would evaporate like smoke.

But for the present, she couldn't move anywhere.

She was determined to avoid her uncle, however, and for three days she pled a touch of the flu that kept her from going down to dinner.

On the fourth evening, she told Ivory she had a meeting at school, and when she left the house she wandered aimlessly along Peoria for two hours in a spring drizzle.

She stayed away from her uncle during a week of steady rain and a week of cornbread for lunch and dinner. But at the end of that week, she sat in her room, listened to the rain, and sighed.

Since she still lived on her uncle's premises, she might as well eat Ivory's meals. Accepting soup and veal cutlets gratis from a Klansman was no more incriminating than accepting a free room over his garage. She had to take responsibility for being there at all.

So she returned to the dining room.

She nonetheless refused to greet her uncle or to make eye contact with him, and when he responded with equal, mute distance, she convinced herself that they'd probably eat together in frosty silence until she moved out.

She was thus caught unaware when he said over blancmange a few evenings later, "I know it hasn't been easy for you to stay here. A young girl needs a more lively house than that of an old bachelor."

She looked at her dessert dish and waited, but, for once, he paused to let her respond, and, finally, when the silence grew too uncomfortable, she was forced to say something.

She nonetheless kept her voice noncommittal and cool as she said, "You've been very kind to let me have a room over your garage. But I didn't mean to stay once I started earning a salary. I always intended to get my own apartment as soon as I could afford it."

He sat silent a moment, and when Black Jack Pershing arched into his lap, he stared down at the black fur.

"I'm not completely unobservant," he said then. "I do understand that you're moving out because I belong to the Ku Klux Klan." He took off his pince-nez to look at her. "Is it that important to you what organizations I belong to?"

"I don't care about other organizations." She finally raised her eyes to his face. "But the Klan—I loathe everything about it."

She was calm but adamant, and as he rubbed the indentations beside his nose, she could tell he'd resolved not to argue with her this time.

"I suppose I hadn't anticipated your moving out so soon," he said at last. "There's a law conference in San Francisco in June, and I was assuming you'd be able to look after the house. It would be a great favor to me to have someone here. I wish you'd consider staying until I get back."

"If I find a room before June, I'll probably—"

"I know I'm a difficult man. I think sometimes the war took away my feelings." He again dropped his gaze to Black Jack Pershing. "I know you don't have any more interest in the war than my wife did, but I'm grateful that you've been polite enough to listen."

His vulnerability stripped away all his defenses, and she felt a wave of guilt that she hadn't tried to be more than polite.

But she immediately hardened herself against compassion by reminding herself how he'd tried to ease his loneliness. "I can't stay in the house of someone who belongs to the Klan."

He nodded.

They sat while the candles dripped, while Black Jack Pershing stretched and yawned.

Then her uncle said, "Klan meetings are once or twice a month."

She waited.

"I'll make a bargain with you."

She hadn't a clue what he was about to suggest, and she continued to study him.

He put on his pince-nez, took them off again. "I'd be willing to forego Klan meetings. At least until June if you'll stay with me until then."

SEVENTEEN

Winter slid imperceptibly into spring.

Persephone brought Zacharia's jonquils, then his irises, to school and distributed them to every classroom. "That man has got two green thumbs."

The sixth graders argued over who got first use of the yellow crayons to color daffodils, who got the purples and blues for the irises. Vivian Green didn't demand either but sat by the window watching Nelson Flowers on the playground with his class. When she began drawing his portrait in red, his quicksilver eyes took on fiery crimson effervescence, and the gouge in his cheekbone narrowed to a gallant saber scar.

"You can have this sketch, too, if you want, Miss O'Brien."

Berneen didn't exhibit this sketch in the office before she took it home and tacked it on her ceiling.

Nor did she admit, even to herself, that she gazed at it too long every night when she went to bed.

Ja. Ja. Ja.

"All right. Remember, y'all, we're meeting at Standpipe Hill rather than at school tomorrow." Caroline paraded down the hall, reminding everyone for the third time, "There's no school, so you can sleep late. But not too late. We're starting the picnic at ten o'clock."

She'd agreed to meet Berneen at nine, and Berneen dutifully arrived on the hillock, carrying the heavy bowl of potato salad Ivory had made that morning and covered with a tea towel.

Caroline was nowhere in sight, but as soon as Berneen reached the stand of elms, she saw Nelson Flowers.

He'd already set up tables and had anchored the tablecloths with smooth, evenly spaced stones. He'd told Persephone, who organized the food, that he'd bring a sugared ham from York's butcher shop, and Berneen saw it, wrapped in its cloth bag, on a platter.

"Miss O'Brien. I wasn't expecting anyone else this early." He nodded at the great bowl she held. "I didn't realize you could cook."

Since she hadn't done the work, she couldn't very well take credit for it, but neither could she acknowledge that her uncle's cook had done the boiling, chopping, and mixing, so she mumbled, knowing she sounded completely addled, "It's not anything cooked. It's cold potato salad."

"*Tres createur,*" he said.

She moved woodenly to place the bowl on the table

beside the ham and stood awkwardly in the speckled shade, not able to unscramble her brain.

After what seemed to her a very long time, Nelson Flowers said, "Here comes Miss Mankiller. Now no one else will get a word in edgewise."

Berneen glanced at him. But he was merely watching Caroline—followed by two fifth-grade boys—trudge up the incline. The boys' arms were loaded with bananas.

Caroline wore a great floppy-brimmed straw hat, banded and tied under her chin with a turquoise satin ribbon that matched the stones in her necklace, and as she held up her long skirt to labor up the slope, she called gaily, "My Aunt Belle got such a good buy on bananas at the Welcome Grocery, I had to commandeer some help to bring them."

The two boys each cradled what appeared to be an entire banana stalk, and when Caroline directed placement of the huge bunches on the table, the yellow smell of ripe fruit overtook the glade.

"I brought plenty for the whole school. And that's going to be more than enough pork for everyone," she said toward the ham. Then indicating Ivory's bowl, "Is this your potato salad, Berneen? I didn't eat any breakfast to save room for all this food, so I've been starving all morning." She swung to her young helpers. "All right, you two urchins. Run over there and play. None of you are allowed to start grazing until everyone gets here. Berneen, wait until you see the prom dress Aunt Belle's making for my cousin Oralee. Did I tell y'all she's sending Oralee to Fisk next fall? She's going to use rent from the Barber Building to pay for tuition and books and the dorm room. Isn't Fisk where you went to school, Mr. Flowers?"

He nodded.

Berneen couldn't help smiling—even as she didn't glance at Nelson Flowers—when Caroline blithely went from the prom dress—whose blue would match the azure decorations planned for the school dance—to a description of the swallow-tail coat her brother would wear to his wedding. "It makes no never mind to that dotty bride of his that he'll look like a penguin. That girl's determined to have the best, and she could care less that her daddy'll go in hock for years for this wedding. Oh, look, here's Persephone."

Persephone came panting up the street, lugging a quilt and a great iron pot that she'd said would contain turnip greens. Nelson Flowers strode quickly down the slope to meet her.

He said something inaudible to Berneen at the top of the hill as he took the iron-lidded kettle from Persephone.

"You should have made Zacharia drive you over," Caroline admonished loudly as they came closer. "You're going to have heat stroke one of these days trying to act like a bluestocking and do everything yourself. Are those greens flavored with the kind of salt pork Zacharia cuts special?"

"I wouldn't know how to cook greens without that salt pork of his." Persephone wiped her forehead and gave them her glittering gold smile. "I'm not trying to be a suffragette, Caroline. I'm walking because the car wouldn't start this morning."

She gauged the sun and spread the quilt on the shady side of an elm.

Caroline adjusted the hat's ribbon under her chin, then swirled her skirt and plopped down on the quilt.

She also wore the lace mitts of an antebellum plantation mistress over her large hands and rings, and she gestured with one of them. "You two may as well join me. Hanford won't be here for a while, and I'll give you odds he'll want to read us some edifying news story as soon as he arrives. We may as well be settled comfortably."

She proceeded to tell Persephone about Oralee's prom dress, about the wedding tuxedo and the wedding plans for the next hour before Hanford Yarborough climbed the hill.

Berneen was relieved to see that he carried only two large grocery sacks of bread and no newspaper.

"I'll give you odds those are day-old loaves," Caroline said in her non-whisper while Persephone frowned.

"Remember his wife can't cook anything," she warned quietly. "And remember how expensive store-bought bread can be."

Hanford Yarborough may or may not have heard Caroline, but after he gave them each his gloomy greeting and laid the bread on the table, he went to the level stretch of hill where Nelson Flowers was directing a game of Red Rover.

Nelson Flowers had removed his jacket, and the snowy cotton of his shirt showed his broad shoulders and chest, his narrow waist. Since he'd also rolled up the shirtsleeves, the deep scar was visible from his wrist to his elbow.

Caroline began describing the three-tiered wedding cake for the reception, but Berneen found it difficult in the sultry heat to keep her attention on marshmallow frosting and sugar roses. Her gaze kept drifting toward the two lines of children and the child racing across the grass into the outstretched arms and clasped hands of the opposing team.

Nelson Flowers stood laughing and shouting encouragement as each little boy or girl tried to break through the line.

"He'd be a good-looking man except for those scars, wouldn't he, Berneen?" Caroline asked, not quietly enough.

Berneen felt herself blushing to her eyes.

Caroline patted her hand with a lace mitt.

Then she also gazed at Nelson Flowers from under her floppy garden hat. "What do you think, Persephone? Do you suppose Mr. Flowers has the same kind of crush on Miss O'Brien that she has on him?"

EIGHTEEN
·················

"Can you believe it's the end of school already? Didn't this year go fast? Faster than you believed possible? Did you imagine you'd have this much fun when you showed up at Liberty Elementary last August?"

Caroline balanced on a stepladder, attaching the strings of silver stars to the ceiling of the high school gym while she grinned down at Berneen.

Berneen's class had taken it upon themselves to make the yards and yards of required blue paper chains as their contribution to the end-of-school prom, and Nelson Flowers had driven the cardboard boxes to Booker T. Washington in his Norwalk, while Berneen and Caroline had walked the few blocks from Liberty to hang them.

A slim, young high-school teacher, whose name Berneen hadn't caught when Caroline introduced her, was busily setting out a punch bowl and punch cups and frowning at Caroline and Berneen on the gym floor in their stocking feet, shoes off to protect the polished wood floor.

Her scowl seemed to deepen whenever she focused on Berneen's short skirt.

"You brought that jet beaded dress to wear to the dance, didn't you?" Caroline threaded another star and dangled it beside the last. "I put my new dimity in my classroom so I wouldn't have to go home to change either. I warned Daddy I wouldn't be home until late, late tonight. Everyone in town is coming, and I heard Mr. Flowers tell Persephone he wouldn't miss this dance for the world."

Berneen felt another of the flushes that were becoming all too common to her whenever someone mentioned Nelson Flowers. She looked quickly around.

He wasn't anywhere in sight.

She swallowed nervously and said in a low, strained voice, "I got the impression that Miss What's-Her-Name with the punch bowl is angling for him."

"It makes no never mind what she's angling for." Caroline had a way of not noticing Berneen's consternation.

"He's probably coming to dance with her." Berneen held up another silver star.

"Girl, she's not his type at all."

Caroline attached the star, leaned back to survey her handiwork, then glanced out the high gym window. "Here comes Hanford at a gallop. Oh, Lord love a duck! He's got a newspaper."

A few seconds later Hanford Yarborough burst through the auditorium door.

He wriggled his single eyebrow in great agitation as he rushed onto the gym floor, neglecting to take off his shoes. "Have you seen Nelson?"

"He's in the school somewhere," Caroline said grandly

from her ladder. "Miss O'Brien can go look for him if you want him in such a hurry."

"No, I—" Berneen started to protest.

Just then Nelson Flowers came in from the other side of the gym.

Berneen noticed the high-school teacher patting her hair and tugging her shirtwaist belt, but Nelson Flowers didn't seem to notice her.

Hanford Yarborough went to him at once. "Nelson, this issue of the *Tribune* just hit the streets. The sheriff has arrested a shoeshine boy for attempted rape."

Caroline jumped adroitly from the ladder. "Who was he, Hanford?"

Nelson Flowers asked at the same moment, "Where did the police take him?"

"He's down at the courthouse. They're just booking him, so there's nothing anybody can do right now but wait."

"I don't think we can afford to wait." Nelson Flowers looked at his watch. "When did they take him into custody?"

"An hour ago."

"Then a mob hasn't gathered too much strength yet."

The high-school teacher disappeared as if she didn't want to hear any more about the subject.

"Who was the man they arrested, Hanford?" Caroline shouldered between him and Nelson Flowers.

"There won't be a mob, Nelson," Hanford Yarborough said around Caroline without answering her. "But if he did rape a white girl, then—"

"Then he won't make it to a trial. He'll be dead before they indict him."

"Who was it?" Caroline demanded again.

Hanford Yarborough glanced at her. "Some boy who worked at the Drexel Building. He attacked the elevator girl."

Berneen's throat constricted.

"What was his name?"

Hanford Yarborough ignored her and grabbed Nelson Flowers' arm. "You aren't going to do anything rash, are you?"

"I won't do anything rash if the sheriff keeps the white mob away from the jail."

"I tell you, there won't be a mob," Hanford Yarborough repeated. "Sheriff McCoy knows what he's about. Mob violence is bad for business. He won't let anything happen to the boy."

"He didn't stop the tar-and-feather party."

"That was different. Those were white men."

"I'll call a couple of veterans to make sure nothing happens. We won't stand still for a lynching."

"You're not taking a gun, are you, Nelson?"

"I don't think that's something you want to know, Hanford."

"You'll get us all in trouble."

Nelson Flowers merely looked at him a moment before he turned and went out.

"Guns never help any situation," Hanford Yarborough said forlornly as he followed Nelson Flowers.

Caroline clutched Berneen's arm as she stooped for her oxfords. "Get your shoes on. We've got to get down to the courthouse."

"I know."

And she knew as well what Caroline would say even before she added, "It's Diamond Dick they've arrested."

NINETEEN

. . . .

An uptown tower clock bonged five, the air settled into its most sluggish time of day, and Berneen edged Caroline into the courthouse shade. She spotted a few other women, mostly white, at the fringes of the crowd.

Some of the women gave away their social status by having forgotten to remove their aprons when they'd rushed from their kitchens, and some of the pale blond ones—whose economic class was buoyed by the presence of servants—had obviously been shopping with their cooks when they'd stopped on their way home to observe the excitement.

Everyone watched Sheriff McCoy, a tall, bony man with a handlebar mustache, who blocked the courthouse door. He'd pushed his cowboy hat back from his high-planed forehead and now he unbuttoned his coat to show the brass star on his vest. "All right now. It's time for you people to go home for supper. All of you."

He scanned the white crowd—which seemed to Berneen to number about fifty men and a dozen women—before he looked at the four black men behind Nelson Flowers. "There ain't nothing to see here. Nothing's going to happen. There ain't a reason in the world for any of you to be hanging around."

Berneen tried to gauge the mood of the assembled people.

At the moment, everyone stood calmly, talking in low murmurs, and she wondered if they'd seen the *Tribune* or if they'd merely gathered out of curiosity. Since the Drexel Building was only a few blocks away, some of the men in bowler hats and string ties might even be out-of-town drummers looking for a little entertainment.

But as she listened to the muttering and watched the scowls directed toward Nelson Flowers and his companions, she knew the mood could change any second.

Sheriff Wilbur McCoy had blue eyes with a strange aquamarine tint, and they blinked near-sightedly while he tugged on his mustache and said, "I want you boys to know that the courthouse elevator is stalled on the third floor. I had my deputies put it out of commission. You'll have to climb three flights to reach the jail proper, and Deputy Jessup's got orders not to open that stairwell door. Not for nobody."

Caroline had pointed Deputy Jessup out to Berneen one time on Greenwood Avenue, and she remembered him as a light-skinned black man who sported a handlebar mustache identical to Sheriff McCoy's.

"That boy's in our custody, and that's where me and Jessup aim to keep him."

The sheriff had obviously selected his second-in-command with care, and he squinted at the group around Nelson Flowers to make sure they appreciated his diligence. "So all of you may as well go on home."

"How come you're protecting the boy who attacked Sarah Page, Sheriff?" a man on the far side of the street yelled.

The blue-green eyes tried to search out the heckler as one of the black veterans said as loudly, "No one knows whether he attacked the girl or not. That's for a jury to decide."

A hush fell over the street, and everyone waited, frozen in place, as if a motion picture projector had stalled.

Then Wilbur McCoy broke the spell by shifting his stance and moving away from the courthouse steps. He cleared his throat and spoke directly to the small knot of men from Deep Greenwood. "That boy'll be all right here tonight. Why don't you people come back in the morning?"

Another moment of breathless quiet dropped over the street and lasted until Nelson Flowers asked softly, "Are you sending everyone away, Will? I'd hate for it to be just us."

The sheriff's sharp face took on the hue of a late after-noon horizon, and his near-sighted eyes flickered nervous-ly. "Sure, I'm sending everybody away." He deliberately tucked the flap of his coat aside to show the holster low on his hip, belted around his waist and strapped to his leg. "All right, now. Everybody go on home."

When no one moved, he glanced around, seeming baf-fled about what to do next.

"We're willing to be deputized if you need us to break up the crowd," Nelson Flowers offered.

The sheriff's flush deepened. "I don't need no help. These boys are leaving." He increased his volume. "If I have to start running people in for loitering, I damned sure will. I got plenty empty cells up there on the third floor. Go on now. All of you. Don't be standing around."

The stasis lasted a long moment.

Then, as if the crowd took pity on him, people began to move away.

The grumbling of the white men and women grew louder and their glances back at the sheriff and the courthouse grew hostile, but nonetheless, in groups of three and four, they began to wander up Main Street.

Berneen tugged Caroline's sleeve. "Let's go on back to school."

They crossed the railroad tracks and could see Liberty School before Caroline said sorrowfully, "But I'll give you odds there won't to be a prom tonight."

The old janitor—knowing most of Greenwood was preparing for the gala end-of-school party—had left all the electric lights blazing and all the doors unlocked. Caroline and Berneen reached the brightly lit little building and, out of habit, went down the hall to Persephone's room.

Caroline wrestled the window open and looked out on the playground. After a few minutes, she said, "I just hope they get Dick out of the jail before anything happens."

She glanced at Berneen, and Berneen quickly buried the thought that Sheriff McCoy himself was probably a Klansman as she said, "If everyone lets the sheriff do his job, everything will be all right."

"Mr. Flowers thinks there's going to be a riot."

"I know." She tried to sound confident as she added, "But maybe he's wrong."

They watched the orange sun begin to sink behind the three-story buildings on Archer.

Finally Caroline shook herself. "This silence is giving me the willies. Let's go up to my room. We can see the railroad tracks from there at any rate. Do you think we'll know right away if something happens?"

"Of course," Berneen said, not at all sure.

It was a strange sensation to be climbing the stairs beside a quiet, thoughtful Caroline, and when they reached Caroline's room, where the new dimity dress hung beside the blackboard, Berneen felt a terrible sadness.

She averted her eyes from the party dress.

It was as if days had passed since they'd been happily affixing silver stars in the high-school gym.

Caroline went directly to the windows and shoved aside the jars of ivy. Tendrils that had attached to the ceiling broke loose and dangled over her head. "Do you suppose Dick's really guilty of attempted rape?"

"You know he isn't." Berneen used her stoutest voice. "No one—especially not Dick Rollins—would be stupid enough to try to rape a girl in an elevator, in the middle of the day, in a crowded uptown building."

She didn't add that she knew the building well because she'd passed it—and Diamond Dick—nearly every morning for the past nine months.

Caroline exhaled. "I didn't think he would."

They leaned on adjoining windowsills while the sun dropped below the skyline. They tried to make conversation, but after a while even Caroline couldn't seem to find anything to say. The haze of sunset gathered like thickening ash.

Then the front door opened, and they both listened intently.

But no footfalls carried up the stairs, and when Nelson Flowers abruptly appeared in the doorway, they both started.

"I wondered who was here," he said.

"We brought clothes for the party," Caroline began. She stopped and inhaled before she added, "We didn't change since we didn't think there'd be a dance tonight."

He looked blank a second before he said, "Oh, yes, the prom." Then, "*Mais non.* I don't think there'll be a dance at Booker T. Washington tonight."

The front door opened again and Hanford Yarborough's anxious voice called, "Nelson?"

"Up here."

Dragging footsteps ascended the stairs, and Hanford Yarborough shuffled into the room. Deep worry lines etched his forehead. He seemed much older than he had that afternoon. "Eule Jones telephoned to say that everyone had left the courthouse and that everything was calm."

Nelson Flowers studied him. "But then you heard more news, didn't you? Things are no longer calm, are they?"

His face puckered into walnut creases of melancholy. "Eule called again a few minutes ago. Circumstances are changing."

"And?"

"Not for the better I'm afraid."

Nelson Flowers controlled a gesture of impatience.

"I want to emphasize that sometimes it's not necessary to act, Nelson. Sometimes it's best not to do anything, especially not something rash."

"I understand. What did Eule say?"

"He wasn't sure how to interpret what might be going on, but—"

"Just give me the bad news."

"He thinks that since it's getting dark a crowd is forming at the courthouse again."

Nelson Flowers tensed.

"McCoy's begun deputizing some of the men."

Nelson Flowers muttered a sharp expletive in French. Then he swung his three eyes to Berneen and Caroline. "I want you two to stay here until we see how things play out. It may be too dangerous to be out on the streets."

Hanford Yarborough held up a placating hand. "You know how excitable Eule is."

"If you think your wife will be all right, Hanford, I'd like you to stay here with Miss O'Brien and Miss Mankiller until I get back."

The gray eyebrow dipped, leveled again. "I made sure my wife's brother could stay with her before I came looking for you."

"Good. Turn out the lights. And stay upstairs."

"Are you carrying a gun?"

Nelson Flowers didn't answer.

"Negroes handling guns only anger white folks."

Nelson Flowers gave him a tired glance, but he merely repeated, "Just stay here for the next couple of hours."

And he was gone.

TWENTY

A long time seemed to pass until Hanford Yarborough said, "I'm sure there won't be any trouble, but I suppose it's advisable to do as he suggests."

"I'll get the lights downstairs," Caroline agreed at once. "I need to call home. Daddy's like you, Hanford. He doesn't hold with firearms, so I know he won't go out, but I can't vouch for my brother Teddy."

Berneen followed Caroline, but she stopped in her room to glance sadly at the beaded dress before she snapped off the lights.

The jet and the empty playground gleamed sadder yet in the thickening twilight.

Had the children been warned there wouldn't be a dance? Had anyone told them the Greenwood community wouldn't be turning out after all? Had someone told them all to remain indoors?

Did dreamy Sam Rollins know his older brother sat in a

jail cell that might be rushed by a lynch mob at any moment?

Had someone told Vivian Green not to go into the street? Had anyone told her Aunt Lily to stay away from the stews tonight?

She returned to the now-dark hallway and felt her way downstairs.

Caroline had already extinguished the lights in the office, and as Berneen passed the room, on an impulse, she stepped inside.

She listened to Caroline's footsteps going from class-room to classroom down the hall, then she grabbed the telephone off the desk.

She could feel the clamminess of her hand on the receiver as she peered at the numbers and dialed. The ringing hummed across the line.

Where was Ivory? Where was her uncle?

It was taking too long. Caroline would be coming back any second.

She took the receiver away from her ear and had nearly hooked it into the stirrup on the pedestal when she heard, "O'Brien residence."

She quickly raised the receiver again. "Ivory, is Uncle Quinn there?"

"No, miss."

Berneen swallowed. "Will you tell him I called and that he should—"

"Oh, wait, miss. Here he is now."

After an interminable pause her uncle said, "Yes?"

"Uncle Quinn, listen to me. You have to stay home tonight."

"I was just going down to the office to—"

"No. Don't go out. Promise me you'll stay home. Keep Ivory from going out, too."

"She's catching the bus to Langston tonight."

"Warn her not to go anywhere near the railway station. There's going to be trouble at the courthouse."

"Can you tell me—?"

She heard Caroline approaching, and she hung up.

She swung quickly around the desk to meet Caroline at the office door.

"That's it," Caroline said. "We're in the dark. Literally. Now what do we do?"

"I think we wait," Berneen said. Her voice shook.

And as she trailed Caroline's ghostly white dress up the stairs, she began to heap blame on herself for her lapse.

Why had she felt obliged to call her uncle?

Why had she brought up the courthouse?

Her uncle agreed to stay away from the Klan until June, but since it was now May 31, perhaps he'd feel he'd already kept his bargain. Perhaps he'd alert his fellow Klansmen, then don his own white hood—and it would be all her fault when Nelson Flowers, with his little band of veterans, came face to face with an overwhelming mob of masked vigilantes.

She went with Caroline into the classroom. The moon began to appear, and she and Caroline stood at the window to watch for what seemed an hour or more. Clouds drifted across the moon as it rose higher in the sky.

Every light in Greenwood had been extinguished. Moonbeams alone lit the streets.

How different the evening had become from the one she'd anticipated.

Every half-hour or so Caroline would exhale and murmur yet again, "I hope nothing's happened at the court-house."

Berneen would glance at her profile and produce yet another reassurance. "We'd hear if something went wrong."

Finally, Caroline said, "You don't think the mob has already dragged Dick from the cell and torn off his clothes and—"

"Caroline, don't."

Hanford Yarborough spoke behind them. "Now, Miss Mankiller, let's not paint this incident any more melancholy than it is."

"Oh, Hanford." Caroline's cry held enough despair to silence even Hanford Yarborough, and Berneen touched her sleeve.

They looked across the square of moonlight on the floor toward the moonlit playground, and Caroline calmed her-self enough to ask, "What time do you suppose it is?"

Hanford Yarborough extended his pocket watch into the block of moonlight, and the watch face glittered. "A little after midnight." He waited a few seconds and added, "Nelson's been gone more than four hours. I think we can assume everything's calmed down."

As he finished the sentence, a vehicle accelerated past the school.

A rebel yell howled into the night, three sharp reports sounded, and three bullets cracked against the front of the building.

Running feet pounded along the sidewalk. More cars and trucks sped past.

More yells split the roar of engines and the squeal of tires.

Another gunshot rang out, and almost simultaneously a

window burst apart downstairs. Glass crashed into the room below with a thunderous splintering.

Caroline grabbed Berneen's hand and they listened to the motors and the shouts recede.

A door downstairs banged open and slammed shut.

In the darkness, Caroline's hand crushed down on Berneen's.

Nelson Flowers came noiselessly into the room.

He was jacketless, and in the moonlight, his white shirt hung eerily isolated, headless. "You two, get away from that window!"

The shirt advanced into the room, rising and lowering to the sound of heavy breathing, and as it reached the moon-lit patch, Berneen could see Nelson Flowers' face emerge above the collar. His scarred cheek glistened with sweat.

"Nelson, are you all right?" Hanford Yarborough said from a dark corner.

"I'm all right." He took another deep breath and moved cautiously to the window Berneen had just vacated.

The pistol in his hand glittered.

"What happened?" Hanford Yarborough whispered. "Is Dick all right?"

Nelson Flowers motioned for silence with the hand holding the gun.

He surveyed the playground from the shelter of the wall another moment before he said, "McCoy and Jessup took him out the back way. No one in the crowd suspected, so they got him away safely."

He retreated from the window, moved closer to Berneen, and she could feel the heat of his shoulder, could detect the residue of starch in his shirt.

"Has everything calmed down?" Hanford Yarborough

whispered more urgently. "If it's not too late, we can talk to the white folks."

"It's too late, Hanford. There must be five hundred men surrounding the courthouse. As soon as they discover McCoy got Dick away, there'll be no stopping them."

"I knew if you went down there carrying a gun, there'd be violence."

"It wasn't the guns, Hanford." After a few seconds he continued in a low voice, "Eule Jones was close to the front, and one of the deputies made the mistake of ordering him to put down his pistol. Eule had taken that gun from a German soldier in France. He wasn't about to hand it over to some peckerwood from his own hometown."

The rasp of his breathing hung in the air, and he returned to the window.

"Somebody grabbed for the gun, Eule shoved back, and some of the others jumped in. A shot was fired. Nobody was hit, but the fact was that a black man had pulled the trigger."

"Nelson, I warned you those hot-headed veterans of yours would bring the Klan down on us all."

Nelson Flowers stared out the window.

"I warned you, Nelson."

"And your warnings were justified, Hanford," Nelson Flowers agreed grimly. "Look out there."

TWENTY-ONE

he three of them hurried to the windows again, and Berneen was jostled into Nelson Flowers' sleeve. Her arm was pinned against the heat of his shirt. Her cheeks and forehead flushed at the unexpected touch, and she couldn't help noticing the warmed-stone smoothness of his arm beneath the cotton, even as she stared out at the orange light suddenly appearing in the valley of dark railroad tracks between Greenwood and uptown.

Black squares of unlit buildings became silhouetted against the orange glow as if the sun had started to come up again.

Berneen tried to ignore everything but the strange illumination. She tried to forget that she stood so close to Nelson Flowers while the rooftops became distinct, while the dark mass of buildings rose against the light. It reminded her of the cutout of a paper town pasted on a lampshade.

"What is it?" Caroline seemed restored now that she knew Diamond Dick had been secreted safely away.

"They're setting fire to the buildings along Archer."

At that moment, a yellow tongue of flame, like the afterthought of a candle, leapt into the night. It appeared and disappeared so quickly, so completely, that Berneen thought for a moment she'd only imagined it.

Then separate sprigs of bright saffron and gold fire spurted from the building rooftops. Runners of flame bounced up, pirouetted briefly, receded.

The scent of burning wood wafted in the open windows, along with the familiar sound of logs crackling in a fireplace. Tracers of embers sprayed from the dancing peaks of yellow fire, and transparent threads of smoke gathered into columns that drifted across the face of the moon.

A great sheet of flame abruptly burned through the smoke.

"That's the Dreamland Theatre!"

Berneen could almost see the theatre seats blaze, one wooden row catching and spinning flames to the next while the red stage curtain dripped velvet fire and the movie screen split into blackened shreds.

Blue flames centered the golden fires that careened from the theatre to Williams' Confectionary and York's butcher shop. Ashes the size of leaves floated upward. The smoke browned in the moonlight as roof tar ignited.

Sudden gunfire came from the roundhouse and the railway station.

"Get back!" Nelson Flowers grabbed Berneen's shoulder.

No more than a second passed before another volley punctured the snap of the fire.

"A stray bullet could easily come this far! All of you, get down!"

Nelson Flowers pulled Berneen further back, and everyone dropped to the floor beneath the windows, enveloped in the scent of burning toast and meat.

Berneen listened to the gunshots that had no pattern, no rhythm, that paused for a moment before they began again in irregular metallic barks. It was as if errant boys were loading and aiming cap-pistols, playing cops and robbers in the street.

But in the surreal semi-darkness that throbbed with fire-light, she could hear the thud of timbers, the crash of collapsing walls, reminding her that it wasn't a game.

Nelson Flowers occasionally got up from his knees to monitor the burning street. "No one's fighting the blaze. The mob must be keeping the fire hoses out of Greenwood. We'll have to get out of here soon."

The pop of the flames seemed abruptly louder, closer, while time inside the classroom seemed to stop.

The dark treetops over the playground began to separate themselves from the fading darkness, and a timid pink tint washed into the sky.

Caroline whispered, "What time is it, Mr. Flowers?"

In the haze of the room, Berneen saw her, leaning against the wall, hugging her ankles, and watching Nelson Flowers.

"Around five."

The loud blast of a whistle suddenly pierced the dawn.

Nelson Flowers stood up cautiously.

Then he stepped back and pulled Berneen to her feet. "We waited too long."

As Berneen wove upright unsteadily, too conscious of Nelson Flowers' hand on her bare arm, she caught sight of the men between the ruined buildings. Shielding themselves in the billows of smoke, dozens of them at a time scrambled across the tracks and surged onto Archer.

They wore ordinary work clothes and slouch hats, not white sheets or hoods, but as they ducked around blackened sections of brick left standing and darted between smoldering ruins, wielding shotguns, baseball bats, and lengths of two-by-fours, there was no mistaking their intent.

Nelson Flowers didn't let go of Berneen as he reached down for Caroline. "Let's get the hell out of here."

Morning light filtered through the gray smoke to expose tumbled clothing from dry-goods stores, gutted chairs and sofas from hotel lobbies, boxes of fruit emptied into the street, metal ice-cream chairs and tables stomped, bent, and melted in the rubble.

Hanford Yarborough raised himself stiffly and peered horrified from the window. "We have to stop this insanity before it's too late!"

He stood motionless for a moment. Then he bolted from the classroom.

Nelson Flowers hurried Berneen and Caroline into the hall while he shouted, "It's already too late!"

Hanford Yarborough didn't look back as he bounded to the foot of the stairs amid the smoke that was seeping through the broken windows and thickening in the lower hallway. He pulled a white handkerchief from his pocket, sprang to the front door and rushed outside.

Berneen could hear his voice as Nelson Flowers propelled her and Caroline down the stairs.

They reached the first floor just as a series of explosions slammed the front of the building.

Nelson Flowers let them go and sprang to the open door.

In an instant he was back inside, guiding Hanford Yarborough with one arm while he shoved the door shut with the other. "Lock the door!"

The light was distinct enough now for Berneen to see that blood covered Hanford Yarborough's forehead, matted his single gray eyebrow and wavered down his gray sideburns to his celluloid collar.

She managed to snap the lock and jump away just as another thud hit the wooden panels.

Caroline stood frozen at the foot of the stairs.

Nelson Flowers lowered Hanford Yarborough to the hallway floor before he ran to the office and dropped into a crouch under the office window.

He took the pistol from his belt and hit the window glass with the gun butt. As the glass slivered to the lawn, he fired two shots.

He reappeared in the hall. "Those shots won't hold them long. We've got to get out of here."

Caroline hadn't moved. "Is Hanford dead?"

"No, he was hit with a brick." He anchored the pistol back in his belt and pried the handkerchief from Hanford Yarborough's hand. He dabbed gently at the blood. "You'll be all right, Hanford. It's almost stopped bleeding. Now, let's go. As soon as they figure out I'm not going to waste shots warning them off, they'll torch the building."

Hanford pushed Nelson Flowers' hand away and sat up groggily. "You go, Nelson. Take Miss O'Brien and Miss Mankiller. I have to try to reason with them."

"Don't be a fool, Hanford. Wait until things calm down."

"I have to try now."

"They won't hear you. I know how it works in wartime, and this is close to war."

Shots banged into the front of the building.

Berneen and Caroline flinched.

"Don't take a useless risk, Hanford! Make your stand at

the church. They might not set fire to the church with you in it."

Hanford Yarborough struggled to a standing position. "You go on. I'll be all right."

"No, you won't." He stood up as well. "Come with us."

"Not this time, Nelson."

Nelson Flowers nodded. He glanced once at Hanford, and then pulled Berneen and Caroline after him. "Once we get outside, don't stop for anything. No matter what you see, no matter what happens, keep going. If one of us falls, the others keep going."

He herded them to the little door behind the stairs and shoved it ajar with his shoulder. "Remember, don't stop, no matter what."

The air was choking with smoke, the smell of burning wood, and the sweet odor of cooking meat.

The high playground fence sheltered them across the dirt yard, and when they reached the small gate on the other side of the playground, Nelson Flowers kicked it open.

They managed to scurry together across the hanging panel into the street just as another volley of gunshots echoed with finality from the front of the building.

TWENTY-TWO

They emerged into a gauntlet of fire and smoke. The cedar at the corner of the lot burst into hot orange flames and incinerated to scorched branches and twigs in a blink. Oily billows rolled across the sky, and fires roared in every window and door as far as Berneen could see down the street.

They ran by a burning upright player piano. The ivory keys had blackened and peeled, the piano wires had heated red-hot and were twanging apart in the blazing cabinet.

A huge shadow suddenly darkened the street as a thirty-foot wingspan swooped above them, almost tipping the treetops. Berneen stared up open-mouthed as a bi-plane balanced on the smoky currents so low that she could see with exquisite clarity the squared tan metal body, the wooden rudder of the tail piece, the double wings supported by polished struts that gleamed with spar varnish.

It seemed close enough for her to touch the oilcloth covering the lower wing and the ropes anchoring the wheels of cheery red that could have belonged on a wheelbarrow. She could see the pilot's eyes through his goggles as he hunched behind the double machine guns mounted on the fuselage.

The double wings swayed past, and Berneen watched as one of the two bombs attached to the flattened belly of the plane slid free and angled toward the school.

An explosion rocked the street.

The windows of what had been Berneen's and Caroline's rooms blew out, a splash of flame pooled through the schoolyard, spreading like searing lava from the foundation to the boundary of the fence. In an instant the building caught fire.

They ran across brick sidewalks littered with glass, porcelain, and crystal shards that crunched under their feet while they dodged through the smoke around bewildered families herded along by the density of the crowd. Women called children's names, children shrieked for their mothers through the blaze of feather pillows and burning hair.

Berneen knew her veins were ready to pound through her temples, her lungs ready to explode. She knew she'd stopped breathing even while her eyes caught glimpses of beds and smashed tables littering the lawns.

A kicked-in viola lay on the grass with its neck broken.

Red pools on porches and lawns merged with purple and brown stains where blood lay fresh, drying, dried. Parents clutched the hands of screaming children, while lone figures wove through the smoke, keening, cradling shattered wrists and elbows, bones that thrust through the skin. One woman in a blood-stained blue nightgown held her severed cheek in place with her palm.

Some people hurried by in the opposite direction carrying objects they'd grabbed from burning homes. A man in a top hat hugged an enormous silver punch bowl holding wax fruit. Barefoot women in housecoats clung to frying pans and clocks as if they'd saved something precious. A woman in a wool topcoat passed them bundling a child in a length of tapestry.

The air was thick with grease and cinders that paled the sun.

A figure, burned so badly it was unrecognizable as either a man or woman, lay in the center of the street with a charred arm across its blackened skull. It lay in anguished sleep, like someone caught in death by the ash of Pompeii, and Berneen's mind registered the lipless mouth open to rows of gold teeth and one white incisor as Nelson Flowers dragged her past.

An abrupt salvo of shots burped out in quick succession like a rapidly igniting string of firecrackers. The firing was different from the desultory shots in the night and dawn, and the crowd ahead in the smoke fumbled, recoiled, then scattered.

The multiple shots sounded again.

Nelson Flowers motioned Berneen and Caroline down a side street.

But rows of shanties already blazed with the flash of dry kindling, and they had to turn back.

Under the crisped remains of an oleander, a woman lay with a little girl in her arms. They might have been resting, but their eyes were open, and Berneen knew they were both dead.

"It's Vivian!"

Nelson Flowers' hold was stronger than her attempt to pull away from him. "We can't stop!"

They were beyond the child and her aunt in an instant,

and, as they retreated, another crack of machine-gun shots came, one after the other.

"Ah." Nelson Flowers' murmur was hardly more than a sigh.

He loosened his hold on Berneen's arm, and his knees buckled before he pulled himself upright.

"Go on!"

The shoulder of his white shirt suddenly blossomed red as if he'd run headlong into a sack of crimson paint.

Berneen flung her arm around his waist to support him.

"No! Go on!" He tried to stand alone, but as Caroline ducked under his other arm, his legs rubberized.

They managed to hold him up and reach another corner. Berneen saw his house, the green spring lawn, the Norwalk in the driveway. The block hadn't been touched by fire yet, but smoke from the next street already obscured the tops of the oaks.

"You two go. Back the way we came. Stay away from Standpipe."

Berneen was as calm as if she'd been her mother in a hospital emergency room, and she raised her voice next to his ear. "You'll burn up inside the house in a few minutes— if you don't bleed to death first." They stumbled forward together, and she shouted to Caroline, "Put him in the car. We've got to get help."

"Can you drive?"

She didn't have the breath to explain that she could. She merely wrenched open the car door, and they struggled to get him up the running board into the high backseat.

"Lie down on the floor. We'll cover you with this lap robe and try to get you to a hospital."

"Oh, Berneen, the hospital's beyond Standpipe Hill."

She didn't explain she wouldn't try for the black hospital but intended to take him uptown. "We've got to stop the bleeding."

Nelson Flowers didn't argue as he lowered himself to the floor below the seat. She unfolded the robe and threw it over him.

Smoke poured down through the oak leaves as if coming through a sieve. A crack of falling timber reverberated close by and screams echoed from the next block.

Berneen scrambled in the right side and slid across the seat to the steering wheel. "All right, Caroline, I'll work the throttle while you crank. The minute the car starts, jump in."

Caroline shook her head. "I've got to go home, Berneen. You have to take Mr. Nelson on alone." Her hair hung in strands over her silver earrings, and a streak of ash like war paint barred her hooked nose. "I've got to go see if my family's all right."

Berneen nodded.

Then she set the spark and throttle levers in a clock position of ten-to-three, found the loop of choke wire, and signaled for Caroline to grab the crank.

Caroline turned the handle once, twice, again, while Berneen shoved the levers to twenty-five of two, the way Mac had shown her the few times he'd let her drive his car.

"Again!"

Caroline leaned into the metal strut and whirled the crank hard around once more.

The motor sputtered. The car shivered.

Berneen clamped her teeth on her lower lip.

The engine choked off.

Cries of children and women spiraled into the abrupt silence.

"Oh, Berneen! We can't do it!" Caroline raised her head over the hood and shoved at her hair.

"Try again." Berneen reset the levers.

Caroline bent over the crank again.

The engine turned over.

Caroline revolved the handle hard again. Berneen quickly moved the levers.

The motor perked on, held. The car vibrated with a hum that drowned out the fire sounds.

Berneen pulled off the hand brake and pressed the reverse pedal. She backed the car rapidly down the driveway.

"Be careful, Caroline!"

"Good luck, girl!"

Caroline turned and ran toward the back of Nelson Flowers' house, and as Berneen pushed her foot against the low-speed pedal, she saw the white flash of Caroline's dress disappear beyond the red geraniums.

Smoke now filled the yard like a hot settling fog.

Berneen lifted her foot off the pedal and let the motor rev into the next gear.

She sat high above the surging people, but the men and women tugging children by the hands or running with babies in their arms didn't look at the Norwalk. No one seemed aware of her as she accelerated the car down the middle of the street. It was as if they existed in a nightmare of flames, smoke, ripping, cracking sound with no words, no notice.

She tried not to see them either as she bit her lower lip and determined that if she turned onto Elgin, she could possibly cross the tracks and get onto Main before the mob reached that end of Archer. Standpipe Hill with its machine gun lay directly in front of her, and the flames on both sides were already too fierce, too hot for her to try the back alleys or Greenwood Avenue.

She could only hope that Nelson Flowers would still be alive when she got to her uncle's.

Which was the only place she could think to take him.

She turned the next corner and the car wobbled with the effort as it picked up speed. A flume of smoke curtained the houses to the corner, and she shuttered her lashes over her eyes to filter out the haze and see the street.

She swerved the car onto Elgin.

The mob was there ahead of her.

TWENTY-THREE

Men in work clothes, with work boots, suspenders, and shapeless hats, appeared through the smoke. They completely blocked the intersection.

There was no street for her to turn onto, and she saw that most of the men held shotguns or baseball bats.

She knew that despite its height, the Norwalk was too flimsy for her to attempt to gun through them. Half a dozen of them could grab the carriage-like sides and drag the car to a halt. And then they'd find Nelson Flowers.

She took her foot off the pedal and let the car coast to a stop before she reached the line of men.

They stared at her with hard blue eyes.

No one said anything, and she felt as if all sound had ceased. She could no longer hear the roar of flames, the cries of lost children, or the thud of the pistons.

Then one of the men stepped from the ranks and approached her.

"What are you doing down here, miss?" His tone was as hard and suspicious as his eyes, and his finger curled around the rifle trigger while he put his other hand on the brass trim of the car.

She willed herself not to show fear. She told herself to act as if she were facing down a territorial dog as she glanced coldly at the hand. Then she looked back at the man's face and concentrated on the fact that he needed a shave.

"What are *you* doing here?" she said, using her mother's voice again. She chilled her tone to ice. "I wish someone would tell me what's going on. I drove down here to pick up our cook, and I found her house on fire."

Her cold regard and her mention of a servant changed the man's expression at once.

He lifted his hand from the car rim, lowered his rifle, and bobbed his head in apology. "Sorry, miss. We come down to round up darkies and take them to the Fair Grounds. I guess you ain't heard. A black boy attacked a white girl in a elevator uptown, and afterward the coloreds went on a rampage. They been looting and shooting up the place. We come down here to help keep the peace."

She had no intention of disputing his version as she stared coldly down from behind the wheel. "I just wish someone had told Papa there was no need for me to come for Beulah before I drove all this way."

She'd never been called upon to lie so readily, but she could hear that she sounded perfectly calm, perfectly offended.

"Is everyone going to the Fair Grounds? Can I go by later and get Beulah?" she asked icily.

"Yes, ma'am. People can go vouch for their servants. We don't aim to interfere with honest darkies."

Her foot twitched and accidentally nicked the pedal.

The car jerked forward.

She lifted her foot from the pedal, but the car kept accelerating.

The men standing in front of the car jumped quickly aside and opened a path for her.

A lump of fright clogged her throat, but she pretended to frown at the inconvenience she'd suffered, and she kept her chin regally elevated while she felt the eyes of the men staring after her as she drove away.

If only she could make it across the tracks before they realized they hadn't searched the car.

She kept her eyes straight ahead.

The tracks seemed to recede as she approached them.

At any moment one of the armed men could come running after her and stop the car.

There was no way she could gentle the crossing for Nelson Flowers on the floor of the back seat, and she bounced the car across the railroad ties as quickly as possible.

Before she could take a relieved breath, she saw ahead on First Street another dense crowd of men.

As she got closer, however, she could see that this crowd didn't seem angry or threatening, but were behaving as if they'd been let out of school for a holiday.

Men stood on running boards, sat on the hoods, and packed the open seats of the few cars parked along the street. Although most of the men carried hunting rifles or pistols, they merely waved them in the air while they called out jocular comments to office workers hanging from the windows of the buildings. Everyone seemed cheerful and festive.

She could feel them also staring at her, but since she knew women behind the wheel of a car were a novelty, she kept her head up and ignored the stares as she drove by at a steady ten miles an hour. She arranged her expression to indicate she was on some important domestic errand.

No one tried to stop her.

She passed a milk cart with its horse placidly waiting while the mob distributed bottles of milk among themselves. The milkman was nowhere in sight.

She didn't look at any of these revelers either as she maneuvered the car around a paneled hay wagon in the middle of the street.

As she drove by, she glanced down at the wagon bed.

It was stacked high with bodies.

She shuddered and averted her eyes, but not before she'd seen that the macabre load was composed of men, mostly in overalls, who'd been tossed on top of each other like corded logs. Some on the uppermost layer still dripped blood on those below, but most of them had already stiffened in rigor mortis, and their empty eyes stared skyward from dark, vacant faces.

She clenched her hands on the steering wheel to keep them from shaking.

Near the corner of Fourth and Main, she drove past a truck jammed with children, none of whom looked over ten years old. Half a dozen men with shotguns guarded the little boys and girls, who huddled together with little pinched faces. The terror had drained from their eyes, and now they sat with expressions nearly as empty as the dead in the wagon.

There was nothing she could do for them, and she didn't focus on them as she drove by.

She didn't look back as she turned on Peoria, then Fifteenth, and at last she saw her uncle's cedars and his porch ahead.

She pulled the car onto the sidewalk, stamped on the reverse pedal, and turned off the motor. The inertia of the car vibrated as she jumped down and opened the back door.

She flung off the lap robe and saw what could have been a scarlet silk shirt covering the body of Nelson Flowers.

"Oh, Mr. Flowers," she said hoarsely.

She knew she'd taken too long. She was too late.

TWENTY-FOUR

H is body moved.

"I'm still here," he murmured. "Though for a while there I wasn't sure."

He sat up awkwardly and slowly, and the bloody shirt clung to his back and chest. "Where are we?"

"It was the only place I could think of to bring you."

He examined the house as she helped him climb stiffly down from the car. He stood a moment hanging onto the side before he took her arm in a firm hold.

Although she was afraid he might collapse any second, they staggered up the walk side by side to the front steps.

He reached out a hand to the porch column, and she saw that he left a bloody print on the whitewash as he let it go and leaned on her again.

She didn't bother to knock but shoved the door open and helped him into the hall. "Uncle Quinn!"

Had he stayed home as she asked him, or had he gone to

Greenwood last night? Had he been with the mob across the tracks?

And had it been only last night that she'd called him?

The nearest room was the library, and she guided Nelson Flowers toward it while she raised her voice again. "Ivory! I need help!"

Then she remembered Ivory had gone to Langston.

They made it to the burgundy sofa and she helped Nelson Flowers lower himself into the leather cushions. He stared at her, at the room. She watched him register the red glass hand through which the sunlight beamed with the sparkle of fresh blood.

But before Nelson Flowers could ask again where she'd taken him, she felt more than saw someone approach the library door.

She felt more than heard her uncle thunder, "What's going on?"

She glanced over her shoulder.

So he was home.

The discovery left her strangely detached since she was less concerned about him than she was with Nelson Flowers' reaction, and she turned her eyes to him while she said, "Mr. Flowers has been shot."

In her own ears, her voice sounded as cold as the one she'd used on the men lining Elgin Street.

Nelson Flowers continued to stare at her without expression.

"I want you to call someone to come right away, Uncle Quinn. He's going to die unless we stop the bleeding."

When her uncle didn't move, didn't say anything, she looked back at him. "There's been a riot."

"I heard about it."

He examined Nelson Flowers a second before he limped into the room and swept the phone off the desk.

Berneen watched him.

What would she do if he called a policemen rather than a doctor?

She waited without breathing while he dialed.

Then he said, "Is Doctor Rutherford there?"

She took a gulp of air and ran from the library. She was almost astonished to discover that she was still wearing shoes, and she kicked them off as she hurried to the kitchen.

He'd be all right now. They'd staunch the blood and the doctor would come to bind up the bullet wound. Nelson Flowers would be all right.

She opened a kitchen drawer and scooped out the stack of Ivory's neatly ironed tea towels.

Had Ivory gotten away to Langston before the riot started?

She ran to the dining room buffet, dragged out a dozen linen tablecloths, and raced back to the library.

Nelson Flowers and her uncle were poised across the room from each other, exactly as she'd left them.

Her uncle said immediately. "Rutherford, along with every other doctor in town, has gone down to the Convention Hall to take care of the wounded."

She inhaled.

"All right. We'll do it ourselves then." She dumped her makeshift bandaging beside the couch and knelt to unbutton Nelson Flowers' bloody shirt. She flung one of the linen tablecloths toward her uncle. "Cut this in strips so I can use it to tie everything in place."

She peeled the sodden shirt away, and Nelson Flowers flinched.

The fresh wound was a jagged tear in the muscle, from

which thick red liquid bubbled with the steadiness of an opened valve.

"Sit up so I can get the towels on your back, too." She focused her attention on the raw muscle and the blood that gushed across his dark skin. "I think the bullet went all the way through."

She dragged the sleeve down his arm and off his wrist-watch and revealed the healed wound that had left a furrow to his shoulder. She took the Luger from his belt and laid it on the carpet, then wadded the shirt loose from his other arm and dropped it beside the pistol. Her hands shook, came away bloody, and she knew her uncle's Persian rug would be ruined.

The first towels soaked an instant scarlet.

But she kept adding them, pressing them firmly into the wet ones against the wound, until finally the crimson patches began to spot each fresh towel more slowly.

Nelson Flowers didn't look down at his blood but continued to stare from her to Quinn O'Brien.

She felt the telltale heat in her cheeks, but she steadied herself as she held towel onto towel and reached around his back with a tablecloth. She glanced at her uncle and said in cool command. "I'm ready for those strips."

But as he handed her a wad of the torn cloth, she heard herself adding too breathlessly, "This is the principal of my school. You two were both in the Argonne Forest."

They stared at each other.

Then Nelson Flowers addressed Quinn O'Brien in French.

Her uncle started, and Berneen said, "Mr. Flowers fought with the French under General Foch. I'm going to need this in strips, too." She tossed him another tablecloth.

He began snipping, tearing the cloth while he studied Nelson Flowers. He'd nearly finished ripping up the entire tablecloth before he, too, said something in French.

"Of course. St. Mihiel," Nelson Flowers answered.

Quinn O'Brien gave Berneen the next bundle of strips. Then he took off his pince-nez and put them back on again. "That's where I got my leg wound. I ended up in a hospital tent at the edge of the woods."

"A lot of my men died there," Nelson Flowers said. After a brief pause, he added, "Remember the fog that morning? I don't think I've ever seen a fog like that." He spoke calmly, ignoring—or perhaps accepting—the fact that he sat on a burgundy couch covered in blood, that Berneen knelt on the carpet beside him winding strips of a linen tablecloth around his chest and back.

Quinn O'Brien didn't take his eyes off Nelson Flowers, and as if he couldn't help himself, he brought the swivel desk chair close to the sofa and sat down.

"Remember how the German machine guns located us once the fog cleared and how the men started dropping in the mud?" Nelson Flowers said.

Quinn O'Brien leaned forward and placed his elbows on his knees. Finally he said, "My best friend got hit in the chest in that first wave. He fell and his lungs filled up with blood like—" He paused. "I didn't stop to help him."

"No one can stop in an attack," Nelson Flowers said kindly.

Silence filled the library.

When her uncle began to talk again, and the two of them spoke a long time—sometimes in English, sometimes in French—Berneen didn't try to follow what they were saying. She heard the trilled names of places, ranks, and companies, but she concentrated on watching for seepage from her bandages, concentrated on binding and knotting the cloth around Nelson Flowers.

At last she heard her uncle say, "No one understands about the war. I couldn't find anyone to talk to. Too many men didn't get overseas. Too many of the ones who did go over didn't come back."

"*Mais non.* You can't give anyone the experience."

Quinn O'Brien sat motionless a long moment before he said, "I had no idea there were any—" He had the grace to hesitate before he concluded, "—any colored troops in that area when we attacked."

"There weren't any colored troops. Only French ones."

"Then you're not an American."

"I was born in Tulsa."

"Oh."

Berneen noticed Nelson Flowers' voice had become hoarse, that the brown of his forehead had taken on a grayish sheen. "Uncle Quinn, call the hospital again."

Her uncle got up and did as she asked, but when he hung up, he repeated, "There's no one available. They told me again there's been a riot."

"It wasn't a riot. It was an invasion," she said fiercely.

"Don't think about it." Nelson Flowers lifted his hand with the gold watch to stop her.

But she couldn't stop. "They killed Vivian Green and Hanford Yarborough and Persephone. They killed hundreds of—"

"Don't think about it now."

"How can you keep from thinking about it?"

"Shift your mind to something else."

"How can you when the blood and the mud, the killing

and the dying are with you every minute, every second?" her uncle added.

"Because you're one of the living." Nelson Flowers looked down at Berneen as his voice grew weaker. "Because you have to teach the children."

Quinn O'Brien watched him a long time before he murmured, "You're different from other—"

Nelson Flowers gave a small sigh. "—from other black folks? No. I'm afraid not."

He closed his eyes.

"Uncle Quinn, do something!"

Her uncle came around the desk, and the red sunspot from the glass shield fell across his hand. He looked down at it. Then he shook himself. "Abner Drew's a pharmacist. Maybe he'll know someone."

"Go ask him."

He stood a moment as if he might say something else to her, something else to Nelson Flowers, but when the latter didn't open his eyes, he went out.

Berneen could smell the heavy smoke from Greenwood as she heard him on the front walk.

She sat on her knees again beside the leather couch while Nelson Flowers' blood dried on her fingers. The light from the red glass hand shifted and glittered on the Luger.

"Why didn't you tell me?" Nelson Flowers didn't open his eyes.

"I didn't know how you'd take it."

He took a shallow breath. "I don't think I'd have minded."

"I know how you feel about white people."

A small smile crossed his face, and his third blank eye seemed to regard her with kindness. "Not all white people."

He opened his eyes then, raised his slender hand, and seemed about to touch her face, but in mid-air, the hand fell back to the arm of the couch. The fingers curved as if surrounding a transparent ball, and the thumb twitched.

She reached out and grabbed his hand. It was warm and the fingers were firm and strong.

The thick bandaging over his chest expanded with a deep breath, but then it failed to deflate again. His thumb moved slightly, his long tapered fingers contracted around her hand.

The warmth in his palm cooled.

The tension drained from his face. His expression washed away with it, and his eyes closed until only a narrow porcelain rim of cornea showed between the lids.

A clot with the consistency of glue plugged her throat. She wasn't sure she'd ever be able to swallow again.

She hadn't moved from her position on the rug beside the sofa, hadn't taken her eyes from Nelson Flowers' face when her uncle came into the library again.

"Drew wasn't home."

"It doesn't matter." She felt him approach the couch, but she didn't look up. "He's dead."

He awkwardly patted her hair. "I'm sorry."

A sob she hadn't known was inside her chest suddenly ripped through her rib cage.

She could no longer see the body of Nelson Flowers, could no longer see the room or the red sunlight that linked the three of them together.

"His blood is on your hands, Uncle Quinn."

"I wasn't with them, Berneen. You called, and I didn't go."

She sat and the tears flooded her vision.

At last she let go of Nelson Flowers' hand and wiped her eyes. She took a jagged breath. "I have to go to the Fair Grounds and to the Convention Center to see if I can find Caroline and her family and get them out."

He waited a second before he said, "I'll drive you if you want me to go with you. We'll take care of Sergeant Flowers' body later."

She finally looked up at his sobered red face. "You'll have to lie and say that Mr. Mankiller is your butler, that the Mankillers are your cooks and parlor maids and lawn boys," she said as calmly as she could. "If you think you're up to that, I'll let you drive me."

He nodded. "I'll get the car."

She watched him limp away before she leaned forward to close Nelson Flowers' eyes.

She held the lids tightly against the hollows of his eye sockets until she was sure they'd stay shut.

Then she lifted the balls of her thumbs away from his lashes and touched one brown marble cheek with the tips of her fingers. For the briefest of moments, she let her forefinger linger on the pink groove of his old wound.

AFTERWORD

．．．．．．．．．．．．．．．．．．．．．．．．

The worst race riot in American history occurred in 1921 in Tulsa, Oklahoma. In a rampage that lasted from the evening of May 31 to the afternoon of June 1, a white mob looted and burned two square miles of the segregated Greenwood section, trained machine guns on black civilians, and dropped incendiary bombs from a World War I bi-plane on the houses. Over seven hundred people were wounded, and possibly as many as three hundred were killed.

Around midnight on May 31, Governor James Robertson ordered the National Guard to Tulsa to help disarm and intern the inhabitants of Greenwood at the Fair Grounds or the Convention Center. The mob continued to loot and set fires, and when the black citizens were finally released, they returned to a completely burned-out neighborhood.

During the riot, Sheriff Willard McCullough slipped Diamond Dick Rowland (on whom the character Dick Rollins is based) out of town and saved him from a lynch mob. The assault charges against him were subsequently dropped when Sarah Page, his accuser, refused to testify.

Although Tulsa officials assured the nation they would rebuild the area, little was done and for years only shells of buildings remained where thriving businesses once stood. Today, the visitor to Greenwood can find a short stretch of Archer restored, a small museum with a marble monument dedicated to "Black Wall Street," and a long grassy knoll beside the freeway that cuts through the streets that once held Greenwood's mansions.

Representative Don Ross has introduced a reparations bill in the Oklahoma State House of Representatives. The bill is still in committee at this writing, but at long last the people of Tulsa are trying to make amends. Such private agencies as the Tulsa Community Foundation intend to give cash to the survivors and scholarships to the descendants of those who didn't survive.

About the Author

Pat Carr has taught English at Rice, Tulane, New Orleans and several other universities. She is the author of four novels, three nonfiction titles, and four book-length short-story collections. She has received numerous awards and honors, including a writing fellowship to the Fondation Ledig-Rowohlt in Lausanne, Switzerland. She and her husband have retired to Elkins, Arkansas.